ABOUT THIS BOOK

She's a rich witch with deep roots. He's a shifter biker with none. When a passionate fling becomes more, it also turns deadly.

Being a witch isn't all magic potions and conjuring up great outfits, especially when your last name is Augustine. As a descendant of a founding family of Havenwood Falls and granddaughter of a high priestess of their coven, she's been raised to adhere to certain expectations—suffocating and annoying expectations. Dating a biker is the exact opposite of those.

At first, it's an act of rebellion. Ryker "Crusher" Pride, enforcer in Swords of the Infernal Night motorcycle club, is like forbidden fruit. Where she has deep roots in town and a big family, Ryker is an orphan lion shifter who grew up on the streets. His family is the MC—"thugs and outlaws," according to her grandmother.

Ryker's brothers are convinced Harlow will break his heart and return to her side of the tracks. But what started as simple lust grows deeper. Ryker gives Harlow strength to stand up to her family. She inspires in him the desire to settle down and make a permanent home. When tragedy strikes, Harlow makes a rash decision out of love and quickly learns that her magic has consequences—deadly consequences that could cause Harlow to lose Ryker and be banished from Havenwood Falls.

HAVENWOOD FALLS SIN & SILK BOOKS

Also try the signature line, Havenwood Falls, the historical paranormal line, Legends of Havenwood Falls, and stories from the local supernatural college in Sun & Moon Academy.

Stay up to date at www.HavenwoodFalls.com

ALSO BY E.J. FECHENDA

THE NEW MAFIA TRILOGY

The Beautiful People

Clean Slate

Endings & Beginnings

Enforcer (a prequel novella)

THE GHOST STORIES TRILOGY

End of the Road

Havoc

The Triangle (Coming Soon)

HAVENWOOD FALLS

Fate, Love & Loyalty

HAVENWOOD FALLS HIGH

Fata Morgana

LEGENDS OF HAVENWOOD FALLS

Fated Beginnings

STRAY WITH ME

A HAVENWOOD FALLS SIN & SILK NOVELLA

E.J. FECHENDA

To my Hubba Bubba

CHAPTER 1

*H*arlow kept her pace and breathing even. Eyes focused on the road ahead. Sweat dripped down her back as she rounded the bend. Havenwood Falls stretched out before her as she ran down Blackstone Road. Creekwood Estates was to her right. Aspen trees, leaves already turning gold, added to the colorful landscape. Sunlight hit solar panels and twinkled brightly. To the left was the cemetery, and while she couldn't hear them, her sister Taylor said the dead often whispered to her when she passed by the hallowed grounds. Harlow's sister was a medium, though, so she wasn't surprised.

A car that Harlow recognized slowed to stop at the end of Stuart Street. She waved to Amanda George, and the young kindergarten teacher waved back before pulling out to make a left onto Blackstone Road, cutting off a motorcycle. Harlow inhaled sharply when she realized the motorcyclist didn't have time to slow down and would hit the car. Without thinking, Harlow snapped her fingers, and instantaneously, time came to a halt. The car and motorcycle paused, along with a bird flying overhead.

"Shit! You've really done it now," she scolded herself. Resigned to the fact that she had just used her magic in front of a human, she quickly proceeded to manipulate the car, so it completed the turn and was out of the way of the motorcycle. As soon as it was clear, she snapped her fingers, and time resumed.

Hoping Amanda, the human she had just used magic on, didn't notice, Harlow continued her run as if nothing had happened. Unfortunately, the man on the motorcycle did notice and pulled over to the side of the road, directly in front of her. She had heard about Ryker Pride, remembered when he arrived in Havenwood Falls a couple years ago. He was a lion shifter—a rarity in Colorado—and that had created some local gossip. The fact that he was hot and single had added to the gossip among her girlfriends.

Ryker had long, dirty-blond hair that was tangled from the wind. He removed his sunglasses, pinning her in place with smoldering blue-gray eyes. A thick layer of stubble blanketed his square jaw. He wore jeans and a long-sleeved flannel shirt that stretched over massive biceps. But the black leather vest he wore over his shirt revealed who he really was. The Swords of the Infernal Night, or SIN Motorcycle Club, was full of men her grandmother warned her about it. By the way Harlow's body responded just by standing within three feet of the giant piece of man candy, she knew her grandmother was right. This man needed to come with a warning label.

"Nice save back there, Country Club. I owe you one," Ryker said, his voice more like a sultry growl that caused her nipples to harden. When his gaze drifted down her body and he gave her a feral grin, followed by a wink, she knew he noticed. Of course, she was wearing a tight black running shirt over her sports bra and skintight leggings, leaving little to the imagination.

Swallowing hard, she crossed her arms over her chest and firmly met his gaze.

"Country Club?" she asked, narrowing her eyes.

His grin widened. "Just a nickname the boys have come up with. Your pops is some big wig at the club and you work there, right?"

Harlow's eyes narrowed even further. "You sure know a lot about me for never having met before, and I already have a nickname? What's that all about?"

Sure, Havenwood Falls was a small town and her dad was the Director of Member Services at Creekwood Country Club, so he knew a lot of people, but that crowd generally didn't mix with bikers. Realizing she sounded judgmental, Harlow closed her eyes and took a deep breath to center herself. When she looked at the biker again, he had his hands in the air as if in surrender. He straddled his bike, a monster black and chrome machine that looked almost as dangerous as its rider.

"Hey, it's no big deal. My brothers and I take notice of all the beautiful single females in town. You're one of them."

Okay, so he's an ass—a hot ass, but an ass. Judgment totally earned, she thought to herself. Harlow was about ready to tell him off when her phone that was strapped to her right bicep started to ring. She glanced at the screen and saw her grandmother's name. Mathilde Augustine was the matriarch of the family, a leader in the Luna Coven, and she sat on the Court of the Sun and the Moon, which was the governing body of the supernatural community in Havenwood Falls. With a sinking sensation in her stomach, Harlow knew the use of her magic had triggered the wards that surrounded the town. Lately, Harlow's grandmother had been extra everything: nosy, controlling, and protective. Harlow didn't know what was going on, but she had heard whispers about an outside threat.

"Harlow, did you just use a little more magic than usual? Are you okay?" she asked when Harlow answered her phone.

"I'm fine, Grandma."

"Are you sure? Nothing unusual happened?"

"Nope, everything is fine."

"No witnesses?"

"Nope," Harlow lied, and she made eye contact with Ryker, whose eyebrows were raised. Based on his reaction Harlow knew he was able to hear the conversation. Shifters were known for their enhanced senses.

"Okay, dear. I was just worried." Harlow's heart softened, and any annoyance at her grandmother being overbearing vanished. She sounded more like a concerned grandmother than a critical leader. It had been a few months since Harlow got in trouble for using her magic in public, and she was relieved to not be on the receiving end of another lecture—or worse.

"No need to be. I'll see you soon. Bye."

She disconnected the call and reached up to tighten her ponytail, in preparation to start running again.

Ryker's gaze roved over her body before he said, "I can think of some other forms of exercise."

He winked at her and laughed when she rolled her eyes before turning away.

"You wish," she said over her shoulder and began to jog back the way she came.

"Wait!" he called out. "I was just fucking around. Want to go out for drinks or something? I owe you. I'd be a heap of road rash right about now if not for you."

"Nothing happened, okay? You didn't see anything." Harlow waved him off and kept running, knowing it was best to put distance between them.

~

The next morning, Harlow arrived at Coffee Haven to open. The sun was just beginning to rise, but it didn't hold much promise to beat back the cold. The weather in their box canyon town was unpredictable. A front had blown in overnight, ushering in temperatures low enough to make snow possible. The bell above the door chimed when she pushed it open, and she inhaled the fresh aroma of coffee brewing. The manager, Davis George, looked up from where he was placing a tray of scones in the display case. They said good morning, and Harlow jumped in on her opening chores. Davis became the manager more than a year ago, when he and his wife Amanda, the woman Harlow had stopped time for the day before, moved to town. Harlow and Davis had established a routine. Neither was usually talkative in the morning, so they worked well together. Except that morning, Davis had a story to tell, and it was one that made Harlow cringe.

"Amanda keeps going on and on about an experience she had yesterday. She claims it was divine intervention or something." Davis took off his dark-framed glasses and cleaned the lenses with the bottom of his apron.

"Really?" Harlow asked, wiping flour off the counter and pretending to be intrigued while ignoring the sinking feeling in her stomach.

"Yeah, she said you were there. She saw you running, and she waved at you, and the next minute, she said she almost collided with a motorcycle, but it was like time stopped or slowed down. She could see the stubble on his jaw, she was that close, but somehow, she avoided hitting him. Did you see it?"

Harlow chose her next words carefully. "I did see the close call, but I'd say it was just luck. I didn't see anything out of the ordinary."

"Good. I'll make sure to tell her that. She's been obsessing over it. I'm just glad she and Junior weren't in an accident."

"Same here." Harlow left the conversation at that, convinced she had nipped the situation in the bud.

There was a steady stream of business all day—customers eager to warm up with a hot coffee or cocoa. By closing time, Harlow had forgotten about the conversation. She and Davis left together, Davis locking the door behind them. They walked down the sidewalk, waving at Sedona, the owner of the bookstore next door, as she was in the front window setting up a new display. They walked several blocks, past the medical center, and Harlow split off to head up to her house. She hunched forward against the cold wind and burrowed her face in her scarf to keep her nose from freezing. Dusk was already descending; the days had noticeably begun to grow shorter.

She had just slipped her shoes off and hung up her jacket when her phone rang. It was her grandmother again.

"Grandma, what's up?" She walked down the short hallway into the kitchen.

"Imagine my surprise when Letitia Blackstone called me up just now with an interesting story."

"Okay . . . what story?" Harlow pulled out her rice cooker from the cabinet next to the refrigerator and set it on the counter.

"Amanda George was in an afternoon yoga class and couldn't stop talking about a miracle that happened."

Harlow groaned internally and hung her head. The beauty of living in a small town. There weren't any secrets, and of all people to overhear Amanda, it had to be Letitia Blackstone. She ran Yoga in the Vines at NamaStays Inn. She was also the retired matriarch of the Blackstone family, one of the founding families, like the Augustines. The two families shared a long history, and Letitia and her grandmother were friends. "The way Amanda described time stopping sounded awfully familiar, and it was right around the time the wards picked up a surge of your magic. Do you have anything to tell me?" Gone was the grandmother tone.

After breathing out a sigh, Harlow admitted she had used her magic to prevent an accident.

"You lied to me."

"Not really. I didn't think Amanda had noticed, so there wasn't anything to worry about. I'm sorry, Grandma. If I'd known, I would have wiped her memory, as I've been trained."

There was a long pause, and Harlow chewed on her lip. She hoped her grandmother didn't press further. If she revealed she had been distracted by a hot biker—well, that excuse would not fly.

Her grandmother breathed out a heavy sigh. "I have to report it to the Court, Harlow. It's my duty."

"But—"

"I can't show leniency because you're my granddaughter. It will call my leadership into question. I'm sorry. I came to your defense after the incident at the Dirty Knuckle, and it caused a stir. I'll let you know what they say."

Before Harlow could respond, her grandmother ended the call.

"Ugh!" she growled and tossed her phone onto the counter. The incident her grandmother referred to had happened over three months earlier, and she was still being punished for it—even though all she did was defend her friend, Shayna. Although, in hindsight, sending a guy flying across the bar for sticking his hand up her friend's skirt might have been a bit overkill, but she had zero tolerance for gropey fuckers, and the guy had been warned after he grabbed Harlow's ass earlier that night. Unfortunately for her, there was a room full of witnesses and a room full of cell phones, plus the guy was angry and wanted to press charges against her for assault. Considerable damage control had to be employed, and Harlow was called in front of the Court. Because of her grandmother, she had been dismissed with a stern warning. Somehow, she had a feeling she wasn't going to be so lucky this time.

Two days later, just before eight p.m. on Tuesday, Harlow parked her Mini Cooper in front of City Hall. She turned off the ignition and sat in her car, focusing on getting her breathing under control. Thoughts of her friend Aster ran through her mind. Aster and her sister, Reeve, had both been banished from Havenwood Falls for using their abilities in public. Fear rendered her immobile, her hands gripping the steering wheel tight. Aster and Reeve's situation was different; it was really, really public. Harlow hoped for a slap on the wrist. As much as she hated the suffocating confines of being an Augustine, she didn't want to be forced from where she was born and raised.

With a final deep exhale, she stepped out of her car and strode with false confidence down the walkway that led around back of the building, to the special entrance for the Court of the Sun and the Moon. Minutes later, Harlow sat at one of the two tables that faced the elevated dais where the members of the Court had convened. Addie Beaumont sat off to the side, taking minutes. A large mural depicting all of the supernatural species that resided in town provided a backdrop for the court members.

Elsmed Fairchild, the fae representative, spoke first, breaking the uncomfortable silence. His long silver hair was pulled back, drawing attention to his preternatural features: extremely pointy ears and a long, narrow face. So long his chin seemed to touch his chest. His penetrating icy blue gaze held Harlow captive. "Ms. Augustine. Your grandmother tells us you used a considerable amount of magic in public, in front of a human, is this correct?"

Harlow broke away from his gaze to look at her grandmother,

who sat to the right of Elsmed. Her back was straight and hands clasped in front of her. Her expression didn't betray any emotion.

"That's correct. There would have been a terrible accident," Harlow started to plead her case, but was cut off by Lawrence Mills. His sharp voice silenced her.

"This is your second offense, is it not? You received a pass the last time." He cast a severe glance at Harlow's grandmother. Harlow swallowed hard.

"Lawrence, let the girl speak," Sandra Beaumont, Addie's grandmother, said. Mr. Mills huffed and leaned back in his chair, crossing his arms over his chest. "Tell us what happened, Harlow."

Harlow relayed the brief incident, making sure to emphasize that Amanda George hadn't seemed aware that anything unusual had occurred.

"Amanda George, the kindergarten teacher?" Mayor Barbie Stuart spoke up. The mayor was the only human who sat on the Court. It made sense that all species, including humans, had representation. With her height and large build, though, the mayor could have been a supe. Perhaps some giant blood ran in her genes. Add in a sky-high bouffant of cotton-candy-pink hair, and she certainly didn't look like a typical politician.

"Yes, and her child was in the car. When I knew an accident was imminent, I reacted. It was a knee-jerk reaction and not an intentional disregard of the law."

"Hmph," Lawrence huffed again.

"She speaks the truth," Elsmed said, after Harlow felt his presence inside her head probing her thoughts. A sensation she had experienced once before and would never get used to—like the tip of a feather was being dragged across her brain.

"Sounds like your granddaughter needs better control over her reactions, Mathilde," Lawrence said to Harlow's grandmother. "And a reminder of the Luna Coven's role: to use magic to cover up mishaps, especially when a human is exposed—not to create a problem."

"Harlow does understand the coven's role. Remember when she covered up after Paisley Underwood healed that human in public? However, I agree she needs to work on her impulsiveness. The coven will address that. I will see to it."

Harlow ground her molars together to keep her mouth shut. Her grandmother, a high priestess of the Luna Coven, had been trying to pull her into coven business more and more. Harlow preferred to stay on the periphery and do her own thing, but her mishap had just given her grandmother leverage.

"The younger generations have zero respect anymore and lack discipline. I propose we start implementing harsher punishments, or they're going to continue to disregard the law. An example must be made! We have more pressing issues at hand, and if people can't follow the law, then I say we be done with them!" Lawrence glowered from under his bushy eyebrows. He opened his mouth to say something else but he was interrupted.

"You mean my generation, Lawrence?" Michaela Petran chided and rolled her eyes. "Because of these issues you mention, we need every capable witch, which Harlow very much is. I propose she does receive further training, though. I believe that would make everyone happy, Lawrence?" The moroi vampire dipped her head in deference to the elder frost dragon shifter. Harlow silently cheered, thankful for Michaela's support. She was also curious about the issues they were referring to that would require every capable witch. What exactly was going on?

"I propose the three-strike rule should apply. One more incident will be the third strike and grounds for banishment," Roman Bishop added in a bored tone. He straightened the sleeves of his suit jacket and brushed at the fabric as if it were covered in dust. Harlow couldn't see any imperfection, and that was Roman, always perfectly dressed and exuding confidence.

"That seems reasonable. Shall we put it to a vote?" Elsmed motioned. There were murmurs of agreement, and when he called for everyone in favor to say aye, Harlow waited, scarcely breathing, for the Court to determine her fate.

A sigh of relief rushed out of her lungs when all but one member voted in favor. She wasn't surprised Lawrence Mills opposed. She'd heard he was a stickler for the rules and old school. Before she could leave, Harlow had to agree to training, and Mathilde would oversee her progress. Another term of the agreement was that if Harlow used her magic in the presence of a human again, without ensuring memories were altered to cover up the incident, she could face immediate banishment.

After that, she was free to go, and she left quickly, rushing up the stairs, pushing open the door, and stepping out into the night. The cool, fresh air was a jarring transition from the oppressive Court's chambers, and she paused to take a few deep breaths. When she reached the end of the walkway and started to approach her car, she was surprised to see someone waiting for her. Ryker sat astride his bike, which was parked next to her Mini. He was leaning forward, his arms resting on tall handlebars with his large hands draping over top. He was facing her, and she felt the weight of his gaze. She faltered and came to a stop in front of her car. He was parked on the left, and she'd have to pass him to get to the driver's side door.

"What are you doing here?" she asked.

"I happened to be driving by and saw you walking in. Does this have anything to do with the other day? Are you good?"

"Oh." Surprised at his concern, she let her guard down and relaxed. Her shoulders seemed to melt away from her ears, and she didn't realize how tense she had been. "I'm okay. Thanks for checking in."

At that moment she heard her grandmother approaching, recognizing her voice by the almost Southern drawl. Harlow looked over her shoulder to see her grandmother walking with Lawrence Mills. Wanting to avoid her, Harlow rushed over to her door. Just as she had her hand on the handle, her grandmother called out.

"Harlow, I need to speak with you!"

"Fuck," she muttered under her breath, and dipped her head forward, causing a cascade of dark waves to shield her face.

"You can hop on the back of my bike and escape," a deep voice growled from behind her. Harlow let out a sigh. Releasing the door handle, she turned to face Ryker.

"Tempting, but my grandmother kind of has me by the balls right now. I need to hear her out."

Ryker chuckled and shook his head. "Quite the mouth you have there, Country Club." He smirked.

"Sorry, did I offend the big bad biker? I didn't realize you were so sensitive."

Another chuckle rumbled from his barrel chest. "Not at all. I like it."

A throat being cleared interrupted their banter, and Harlow stifled a groan as she looked over at her grandmother who was standing at the curb's edge, eyes darting between her and Ryker. She pursed her lips.

"Harlow, I need to speak to you. Alone." Mathilde directed this toward Ryker, dismissing him with a single word.

"Whatever," Ryker growled and fired up his bike. He backed out of the spot and dipped his head in Harlow's direction. "See ya 'round, Country Club," he called before roaring off, the rumble of his pipes vibrating through her.

Harlow watched him go, enjoying the way his arm muscles bunched as he controlled his motorcycle, instantly regretting that she didn't take him up on the offer of escaping with him.

"Really, Harlow, a SIN member? Since when did you start associating with them? I don't approve and don't think your father will, either."

"Grandma, I don't hang out with SIN. I just met that guy when I saved his ass."

"Well, good. You're an Augustine, and we don't socialize with thugs and outlaws."

Harlow shook her head and pressed her lips together to keep from smirking. Roman Bishop and his brothers had a legendary reputation of conducting business that wasn't exactly on the up and up, and yet Roman sat on the Court. The fact that he was also from one of the town's founding families, wore fancy suits, and lived in Havenwood Heights helped people see past any indiscretions.

"What did you need to talk to me about?" she asked, eager to salvage the rest of her night.

"Are you scheduled to work at the country club Saturday night?"

"No. I'm working during the day at Coffee Haven. Shayna and I are going to grab drinks somewhere after her shift at the medical center. Why?"

"Cancel. Saturday you start your lessons with me, and I'm having a dinner party after. Your attendance is mandatory." Her grandmother spun and started to walk away while Harlow stood there with her mouth hanging open in disbelief. She felt like she was twelve again and being reprimanded. "Be at my house by four and bring something nice to change into. Don't be late!" Her grandmother called over her shoulder and waved her hand in the air, causing the giant moonstone ring she always wore to flash.

Whether it was night or day, the ring seemed to attract any light. Mathilde's long skirt billowed as she walked down the sidewalk.

"Unbelievable. I'm a grown ass witch and don't need lessons," Harlow muttered to herself as she slid into her car and turned on the engine, cranking the heat.

The next day Harlow wasn't working at either of her jobs, and she started the morning off with a latte and some retail therapy.

Harlow breathed in deep, inhaling the familiar, tantalizing smells of fresh coffee and baked pastries. There was always good energy in Coffee Haven, and that's why she liked working there. Strategically placed crystals, live plants, and colorful artwork on the walls, from local artists, kept the atmosphere positive. Her boss, Willow Fairchild, was behind the marble counter. Willow's long silvery-blond hair—similar to her great-grandfather Elsmed's hair and a common fae trait—was pulled back in a ponytail, and her black apron was dusted with flour. She was mixing batter in a large red bowl.

"Hey, what are you doing here on your day off?" she asked.

"I need my fix," Harlow said with a grin and walked around behind the counter to make herself a latte, expertly working the espresso machine. Right before she steamed the milk, she added a drop of vanilla in to sweeten it a little. As soon as it was ready, Harlow took a sip, and even though she almost scalded her tongue, she groaned with pleasure.

"Wow. Just one sip and your mood shifted. Your love for coffee is real," Willow joked, as she poured the batter she had been mixing into muffin tins. Willow was an empath and could pick up moods and energy a person was emitting. "Rough day?"

"You could say that."

"Want to talk about it?"

Harlow looked around the shop at the few customers seated at tables throughout. It was between the early morning and lunch rushes, so quieter than usual. Leaning in closer to Willow and keeping her voice down, she filled her boss in on everything that had happened and recounted her meeting with the Court. She hadn't said anything to Willow earlier, or to anyone else, because she didn't want anyone to worry—or fight her battles for her. Willow would have gone to Elsmed.

"Davis told me about Amanda's experience, but it sounds like she's already moved on. Wait, back up. Who is Ryker?"

"He's the biker Amanda would have hit."

"He made an impression on you," Willow said with a sly smile and a wink, her turquoise blue eyes sparkling. The timer buzzed on the oven. She put oven mitts on before pulling a tray of steaming hot muffins out and setting it on the counter to cool.

"Not really. He's kind of an ass. A real bro type. All muscle and cockiness."

Willow snorted and shook her head as she untied her apron and tossed it in the hamper under the counter. "Your words don't match with what I'm sensing. Your aura lights up like a fireworks display whenever you mention him. You're definitely attracted to him."

"Pft. I am not," Harlow sputtered. Visions of Ryker's muscular body filled her mind, causing a flush to wash over her.

"Uh huh. Sure!" Willow teased. "You can't fool me. I say go for it. Didn't you just tell me last week that you needed to end your dry streak? Bad boys have an appeal. Go scratch that itch, girl!"

Harlow was still laughing at her boss when she left Coffee Haven and went next door to check out Callie's Consignments. If she had to suffer through one of her grandmother's hoity toity dinner parties, she was going to splurge on a new outfit for the occasion. Stepping inside the boutique was like stepping back in time. Callie specialized in vintage. One wall was lined with heavily beaded gowns that sparkled like jewels in the sun pouring in from the large storefront window. Classic denim and leather items that were just as trendy now as they were in the fifties caught her attention, particularly a leather vest that reminded her of a biker who was occupying too much space in her thoughts. She lifted the hanger off the rack and subtly brought the vest to her nose, taking a deep sniff. The rich oily scent seemed almost exotic and forbidden to her, but there wasn't anything special about it—it was just a leather vest.

"Did you just smell that?" Callie asked from directly behind Harlow, making her jump. She had been so fixated she hadn't heard the store owner approach.

"I like the smell of leather," she responded, a little defensively.

"Your newfound love of leather smell doesn't have anything to do with Ryker, does it? I saw you two talking last night." Callie gestured with her head in the direction of City Hall, her long dark brown hair shifting with the movement.

"You know Ryker?"

Callie shrugged. "I know of him. I think he's delivered packages to Ronan. I didn't realize you were friends with him?"

The question hung in the air unanswered as Harlow processed the information. Callie and Ronan were an on-again, off-again couple and had lately been on-again. Ronan Bishop was one of Roman's younger brothers, and Harlow had heard through the coven grapevine that if you needed to procure something through untraceable channels, Ronan was the guy you went to. She shouldn't have been surprised that Ryker and Ronan knew each other, but she was, and a little disappointed.

"I don't know him. We just met the other day. Anyway, I'm here about an outfit." Harlow changed the subject, and soon she and Callie were going through the racks. When she left the store over an hour later, she had a ruby-red dress in one hand and a pair of black leather boots with four-inch spiked heels in the other.

They were an impulse buy after she imagined riding on the back of Ryker's bike, her arms wrapped around his barrel chest and her thighs pressed against his.

It wasn't going to happen. It couldn't. Her grandmother would have a stroke. But the idea of breaking free of her familial obligations, of having a fling with a bad boy was appealing—not that she'd ever act on it, especially since she now had to be on her best behavior. At least with the boots she could fantasize.

CHAPTER 2

On Saturday, Harlow arrived at her grandparents' house located in Creekwood Estates. She pulled her car into the detached three-car garage. There was space since her grandparents owned two vehicles: a Subaru hatchback and her grandfather's baby, a vintage Bentley. Their house was large for Creekwood Estates but small in comparison to the Augustine manor in Havenwood Heights, where they used to live. Harlow's uncle Dominic lived in the manor now with his family.

She grabbed her bag and dress that was on a hanger. The front door opened on its own as she approached, and she warily stepped inside, listening to her intuition that her grandmother was going to test her from the start, and she was right. As soon as she stepped in the door, a baseball went whizzing by, and Harlow stepped back just in time to avoid being pegged in the head. It hit the wall to her left with a thud and rolled to a stop on the marble floor.

"Grandma, what the hell?"

"Testing your reaction, dear. You said it's a knee-jerk reaction to use your magic to stop time but you didn't use it just now to protect yourself. Why is that?"

Harlow set her bag down in the foyer and draped her dress across her arm. "I don't know. I reflexively took a step back."

"I have a theory. Come." Her grandmother turned and gestured for Harlow to follow down the hallway past the dining room to the office. The hallway was wide, and the walls were covered with family portraits and a few landscape paintings of the untamed wilderness, out of which the founding families carved Havenwood Falls. Harlow's sneakers squeaked on the hardwood floors that shone like polished amber.

Her grandfather's presence was strong in the office. His spicy cologne seemed to have been absorbed into the very walls along with faint traces of cigar smoke. Mathilde had recently redecorated, painted the navy walls a creamy white, which lightened the room considerably, but she had kept two large brown leather chairs, which faced the fireplace. The wall behind the heavy walnut desk was lined with built-in bookshelves. The family grimoire was kept in a glass case to protect the brittle pages. Harlow's grandmother crossed the room, and after pushing the sleeves of her heather-gray tunic up to her elbows, she opened the glass case to lift out the grimoire. This book had been in the Augustine family for generations and contained all sorts of spells, incantations, and enchantments. It also served as a genealogical guide. Far more in-depth than a family tree, it contained a written history of each witch's abilities.

"Did you know your great-great-aunt Lucille was able to control time, too?" her grandmother asked as she set the leather-bound grimoire down on the desk and pointed at a page full of flowing handwriting that had begun to fade. "Not only could she stop time, but she could rewind it by a few minutes. Enough to reverse if someone was killed or injured."

"No, I didn't know that." Harlow walked around the desk to stand next to her grandmother and look at the book. There was a note scribbled in the margins next to the name Lucille Augustine.

Reversed time enough so Harvey and Eloise could escape the house fire. Slept for twelve hours straight after.

On the other side of the page, there was another note. Here the handwriting was harder to read as the letters were cramped together near the binding.

Charles was dead, then I changed time, and he was whole again, as if his death didn't happen, except he was altered. Death should remain final.

This last sentence was underlined, and a chill traveled down Harlow's spine as she noted the warning. There was a general rule with magic that one didn't mess with death and try to restore life. Necromancy was considered dark magic. Apparently, altering time to change the outcome of someone's fate bordered on immoral.

"Who is Charles?" Harlow asked.

"He was Aunt Lucille's husband. You will find, dear, that when you love someone, you will do anything to save them. That's not necessarily a good thing, as in this case. Sadly, Charles and Lucille's romance ended in tragedy. As her note suggests, all didn't go well when she reversed time, which brings me to my theory." Mathilde closed the grimoire with a thud and placed the tome back in its case. "You used your magic to lessen the impact of Paisley using her abilities in public last year. More recently, you used your magic to protect Shayna and then you used it to keep Amanda George from hitting that biker. I threw a baseball at your head, and yet you didn't use your magic to protect yourself."

"Yeah, so?" Harlow tilted her head and regarded her grandmother while waiting for her to make her point.

"My point is, I think when someone you know is in danger, it serves as a trigger for your magic. This is what we'll work on. Teaching yourself to slow down and evaluate before immediately stopping time. The incident with Paisley was an appropriate use to protect our people and our town's secrets, but I don't think it was calculated as such, was it?"

"Not exactly," Harlow admitted, knowing it had been another knee-jerk reaction. She just hadn't been reprimanded for it that time, because her actions served the Court.

Mathilde nodded. "We're also going to explore your abilities. I've been wanting to see what you're capable of for a long time. It's only fair to the coven to know what magic we have to call upon if necessary. Now"—Mathilde started walking toward the door—"it's time to get ready for dinner. Feel free to use the guest suite at the top of the stairs."

Stifling a groan, Harlow followed her grandmother out of the office and down the hall. When Mathilde peeled off in the direction of the kitchen, Harlow kept going. Retrieving her bag and dress from where she had left them by the front door, she climbed the sweeping staircase to the second floor and found the door to the guest suite open. Thick carpet absorbed her footsteps as she crossed the room to a king bed covered in a multitude of throw pillows. A restored leather steamer trunk was at the foot of the bed, and Harlow laid her dress across the top before setting her bag on the floor, slipping off her sneakers, and climbing onto the bed.

"Goddess, give me strength to get through another one of Grandma's dinner parties," she said to the canopy that stretched above her. She lay there for a few minutes, enjoying the silence and being off her feet. After working and standing most of the day, she was tired. Her eyes had started to drift closed when the sounds of voices and car doors closing outside caught her attention. Getting up, she walked over to the window and parted the curtain. The driveway was directly below the guest suite, and she recognized her dad's BMW. She caught a glimpse of the top of her parents' heads before they walked up the front steps and disappeared inside.

Harlow quickly changed into her dress, which was a scarlet red and made from the softest silk. The dress had spaghetti straps and was flowy, but not so flowy that it hid her curves. The hem stopped a few inches above her knees, showcasing her muscular calves. She went into the bathroom to finish getting ready. Her hair had been held back in a loose ponytail. Pulling the elastic off set her long dark waves free. She ran her fingers through her hair to set any tangles straight, then brushed her teeth and touched up her makeup. Right before she left to go downstairs, Harlow put on a pair of black strappy heels. A final glance in the mirror on the antique wardrobe was met with satisfaction, not that she expected to meet anyone new at a coven dinner party.

As she descended the stairs, the buzz of numerous conversations grew louder. She followed the noise to what her grandmother still referred to as the parlor. Her aunt Ronya and cousin Gianna were sitting next to each other on the settee, deep in conversation. Her father was holding court over by the bar with her grandfather, flanked by her uncle Dominic and Martin Parker. Each had a glass of amber liquid in their hands, which she assumed was Warded Whiskey, her father's favorite. Harlow spotted Curtis Parker, who was standing somewhat in the corner with his grandmother, Patty Parker. Based on the blank look on his face, Harlow guessed he was bored and needed an interruption.

"Hey, Curtis, long time no see," she said, sidling up beside him and slipping her arm through his. They had grown up together and graduated from Sun and Moon Academy the same year. Since he had started to help out managing Parker's Perfect Placement Agency, the family business his grandparents had founded, it seemed like the only time she saw him was when he came into Coffee Haven.

"Harlow, dear. Don't you look lovely!" Patty Parker said. "Curtis, don't you think she looks lovely?" Patty's smile was a little too big as she stared down her grandson.

Curtis turned his head to look at Harlow, and his brown eyes scanned her body from head to toe. "You look great. That's a fabulous color red. Where did you get the dress?"

"Callie's."

"Of course. I could spend all day in that store. She has amazing things."

Patty beamed at them and patted Curtis on the arm. "I'll let you two catch up," she said before walking away.

"That was weird," they said at the same time, which prompted Harlow to laugh.

"This whole thing is. It's all my family, except for yours."

"I think they're up to something—look."

Harlow followed Curtis's gaze and saw his grandmother and her grandmother talking to each other, occasionally glancing in their direction. The way they leaned in toward each other made them look like two thieves plotting.

"Well, that can't be good."

"You're right. Drink?"

"Goddess, yes!"

They made their way across the room to the bar, where Harlow's father looked at them in surprise. "Sweet pea, what are you doing here?"

"Grandma didn't tell you I was coming?"

"No. Well, she may have, and I might have forgotten or not listened." He winked and took a sip of whiskey. "So, why are you here?"

Harlow sighed and gratefully accepted the gin and tonic that Curtis handed her. "I'm Grandma's latest project. Haven't you heard?"

"I did and wish I had heard about your hearing with the Court from you. Why didn't you say anything?"

"What hearing?" Curtis asked. He was leaning against the bar, the small of his back at the height of the counter. Harlow filled him in on how she had used her magic on a human and as a result had been added to the Court's version of a watch list. Curtis laughed and shook his head. "Can't leave you unsupervised for one minute, can I?" he teased.

Just then her grandmother announced to the room that dinner was ready.

"Where's Mom?" Harlow asked her dad, realizing she wasn't in the room. "I saw you two arrive. And where's Taylor?"

"Oh, right." He sighed. "Your mom's out on the patio. I'll go get her. And your sister is visiting Paisley at school this weekend."

Harlow tipped her glass and drained her cocktail while watching her dad leave. She should have known her mom would have made herself scarce. She and Harlow's grandmother got along as well as two feral cats stuck in a crate together.

"Tonight is going to be so much fun," she muttered and set her empty glass down on the bar.

"Shall we?" Curtis placed his hand on the small of her back and guided her forward.

They followed the rest of the guests into the formal dining room across the hall. A huge candelabra took up the center of the table, and twelve white taper candles flickered as people moved around the table looking for their seats. Harlow found her nameplate and discovered she would be sitting between her grandmother, who was at one end of the table, and Curtis. Curtis's grandmother, Patty, sat on his other side. Curtis held the high-backed chair out for her, and she dropped down onto the upholstered cushion.

"Always the gentleman, aren't you, my boy?" Patty beamed at

Curtis before leaning forward to get Harlow's attention. "He's quite the catch, isn't he?"

"Gram, what are you doing?"

"What? I can't compliment my grandson in front of a beautiful woman?" As if offended, Patty sniffed and turned her head, chin first, to talk to Gianna, who had just taken the seat next to her.

Harlow's parents appeared in the high-arched entranceway to the dining room. The only remaining open seats were across from Harlow and Curtis. Spotting the chairs, they quickly made their way over.

"Hi, Mom," Harlow said with a smile. "You look amazing."

Her mom smiled radiantly in response to the compliment. Wearing a dove gray wrap dress that accentuated her thin waist and with her dark hair twisted into a chignon, Aimi Augustine looked young enough to be Harlow's older sister, not mother. Her skin was smooth and wrinkle-free. Prominent cheekbones helped to keep her skin taut.

"Thank you, honey. You look lovely, too. I was surprised when your dad told me you were here. We didn't see your car in the driveway."

"I parked in the garage."

The small talk continued like that until her grandmother stood up and tapped a spoon against her wineglass to get everyone's attention.

"Thank you all for coming tonight. It's important for families to stick together and stay connected. We're stronger and more united when we care about each other and are involved in each other's lives, which is why I asked you all here. This past year has brought some challenges, and I fear our town is going to be tested even more in the coming months."

This statement prompted side conversations to erupt around the table. Whatever Mathilde knew, she didn't elaborate on.

Perhaps it was Court business, and she revealed as much as she was able to. Mathilde paused and smiled nervously at Harlow and Curtis. She licked her lips before casting a glance at Patty. Clearing her throat to get everyone's attention again, she continued.

"It's essential, more than ever, to close ranks and look out for each other. Each generation tends to drift further away. My grandson, Gallad, is the exception, and his alliance with the witch hunters, through his girlfriend Macy Blackstone, is one that will benefit us. It was less than two hundred years ago when marriages were arranged with alliances like this in mind. Bloodlines and the coven were strengthened as a result. In fact, Del and I are an example of such a successful arrangement." Mathilde smiled down the length of the table to where Harlow's grandfather sat at the other end.

Harlow looked around the room and saw similar confused expressions mirroring her own. What was her grandmother rattling on about?

"Patty and I, being the matriarchs of our families, think that the future of our families and the coven will benefit from such an arrangement. While this may seem archaic and unfair, we all have to make sacrifices for the greater good. We've decided Curtis and Harlow are a good match, and we shall celebrate their marriage in the near future. Isn't that exciting?" Mathilde raised her wineglass in the air to make a toast. "Join me in celebrating this happy news."

The room grew eerily quiet, as if Harlow had stopped time, but she hadn't. The words registered, the announcement took root, and Harlow reacted.

"What?" She shoved away from the table and jumped to her feet, her mouth hanging open in shock.

"Mother, what are you doing?" her father yelled. Looking over at him, she noticed his face had gone bright red. Curtis was in an equal state and yelling at his grandmother while his grandfather, Martin, shook his head in disappointment.

"Grandma, this isn't the 1800s. You can't just marry me off like a piece of property!" Harlow had found her voice and lit into Mathilde. "This is ridiculous, and it's not happening."

"Exactly. How dare you go around us and make decisions about our daughter like this?" Aimi chimed in. "Have you lost your mind?"

"Like my son did when he married you?" Mathilde fired back, and all of the color drained from Aimi's face.

Harlow's hands itched, and she wanted to slap her grandmother for saying that to her mom. Comments like that weren't new. Ever since Harlow could remember, her mom and grandmother didn't get along. Apparently, her grandmother expected her son to marry a witch, but when he left for college, he fell in love with a Japanese exchange student. Her mom wasn't a witch, but she wasn't completely human either. Aimi was a descendant of a long line of itako—blind women who were spirit mediums. While Aimi wasn't blind, she communicated with spirits, an ability she passed on to Harlow's little sister, Taylor.

"Oh, not this again!" Harlow's dad came to her mom's defense, and the shouting match escalated. Harlow glanced over at Curtis to see him looking equally pissed off. His grandmother was crying, and Martin had his arm around her shoulders.

"I'm out," Harlow said to Curtis. "You?"

He nodded, and Harlow, placing her hand on his arm, whispered a spell. Everyone, except for her and Curtis, froze. The room went from DEFCON 1 to complete silence. They rushed out of the dining room and headed for the front door.

"Wait, I need to grab my shit!" Harlow gestured for Curtis to stay and ran as fast as her high heels allowed, up the stairs to the guest bedroom. She tossed her makeup bag in her duffel and

E.J. FECHENDA

zipped it closed. She stuck her cell phone in the back pocket of her handbag and swung that over her shoulder. Curtis was holding the door open when she came back downstairs.

As soon as the door closed behind them, Harlow took a deep breath of the crisp night air.

"Where to next?" she asked.

"Anywhere but here. Drinks?"

"Goddess, yes! Where?"

"I know a place. I'll follow you back to your house, and we'll take my car."

Within seconds, Harlow had punched the garage door code into the panel on the side of the garage. Her bags preceded her into the car and landed on the passenger seat. She backed out and as she drove past the front of her grandmother's house, she released the spell. Her cell phone started ringing before she reached the main entrance to Creekwood Estates. She ignored it. She'd had enough of family for the night.

Pulling into the short driveway next to her house, Harlow parked her car, and Curtis pulled in behind her. The headlights from his Tahoe illuminated the inside of her Mini. With keys in hand, she walked up the small set of steps that led to the porch. Curtis held the screen door open for her while she unlocked the front door and stepped inside her dark house. With a snap of her fingers, she turned on the lamp next to the sofa in her cozy living room. She lived in a two-bedroom bungalow that was just the right size for her. A fenced-in backyard provided a safe area, reinforced with wards, of course, for her familiar, Mamoru, who hopped down the narrow hallway from the kitchen to greet her. Mamoru meant "protector" in Japanese, and he was a beautiful snowshoe hare. While he wasn't a vicious rabbit out of *Monty Python and the Holy Grail*, he thumped a warning whenever he felt a threat to Harlow was near.

"Hi, sweet Mamoru," Harlow cooed, bending over to scoop up the white ball of fur after taking her heels off. She scratched him behind his ears as she walked toward her bedroom. "I'm going to go change," she called over her shoulder.

Curtis had taken off his shoes, too, adhering to the Japanese tradition Harlow had learned from her mom. He draped his suit jacket on the back of the loveseat before sitting down. He stretched his legs out, propping his feet up on the coffee table. "No need to change. What you have on is perfect for where we're going."

"And where is that?" Harlow reappeared and set Mamoru down next to Curtis. She tossed her hair over her shoulder and crossed her arms, waiting impatiently for her friend, who was acting very mysterious.

Looking up at her, he grinned, flashing a brilliant display of perfect teeth. "Have you ever been to Silk?"

Her nose scrunched up as if she smelled something awful. "The sex club? Uh, no!" She snagged a plush decorative pillow and chucked it at Curtis, who caught it with ease.

"It's not a sex club. Well, maybe it is, but it's a regular nightclub, too. Silk is exclusive, but I can get us in."

"Oh, really?" Harlow arched an eyebrow.

"Yeah, I know a guy."

She burst out laughing. "Let me guess, some guy you're fucking."

"Harlow, I am shocked you think of me in that way." Curtis pressed a hand against his chest as if she had wounded his heart. "You're not wrong." He winked and grinned again. "Although fucking is so crass. We're part-time lovers."

Harlow held a hand out in front her. "Do not start singing that Stevie Wonder song!" she warned, and Curtis snorted, startling Mamoru, who hopped down off the sofa and thumped his hind feet indignantly against the hardwood floor before settling into his little bed near the fireplace.

"Can I invite Shayna? We were supposed to go out tonight before Grandma summoned me to her dinner party."

"Of course. I'll text my friend and let him know."

Harlow walked over to the small table by her front door and next to the coatrack. She had tossed her handbag on the table when she came in. Retrieving her cell phone, she saw the notification light blinking. When she unlocked her screen, she discovered she had over thirty text messages and five missed calls. All were from her parents except from her grandmother, who'd left a voicemail. She had no desire to hear that message anytime soon. Ignoring all of the messages, she cleared her notifications so her phone would stop blinking and texted Shayna.

Harlow: Hey girl, still up for drinks but at Silk? Curtis has an in.

She brought her phone with her back to her bedroom, where she eyed the black leather boots she had purchased at Callie's. The weather had turned cooler in the past week and had officially become boot weather.

Harlow went into the bathroom. Her bungalow was small, and the only bathroom was in the hall right outside her bedroom. While she was touching up her eye makeup, adding a smoky effect to enhance the almond shape of her eyes, her phone buzzed. She glanced down at where it was on the sink vanity with trepidation until she saw it was Shayna texting her back.

Shayna was her best friend who, like Harlow, worked two jobs. Between their schedules, they barely saw each other.

Shayna: That's so cool. I can't go. ☹ ER is cray tonight. Working a double.

Harlow: That sucks! I need to go out. Grandma's party was a shitshow.

Shayna: Uh oh. What happened?

Harlow: Nothing except an ARRANGED MARRIAGE BETWEEN ME AND CURTIS!!

Shayna: WHAT?!

Harlow: It's so not happening. We need to talk. Are you free tomorrow?

Shayna: Yes. Lunch at Sakura?

Harlow: OMG Yes!

They made arrangements to meet at noon, and Harlow finished getting ready. Grabbing her boots, she joined Curtis in the living room. Sitting on the edge of the sofa, she put the boots on. They stopped right above her knees and hugged her calves like a second skin, with crisscross leather laces that ran up the back. The heels were at least four inches and the toes pointy. Not the most comfortable, but as Harlow looked in the mirror above the table by her front door, she loved what she saw. There was a glimpse of toned thigh between where the boots ended and her dress began. The black leather and red silk boldly complemented each other. It was an edgier look, and she loved it. She fluffed her hair, which hung in long, thick waves to the middle of her back.

Curtis whistled. "Girl, you're looking for trouble in that outfit. Those boots are fierce!"

"You like?" She twirled once and ended with a hand on her cocked hip.

"If I wasn't gay, I'd be trying to get in your panties," Curtis said, with a flirtatious wink that made her giggle. He stood up and put his shoes and suit jacket on, pulling the keys to his car out of one of his pants pockets. "Are we picking up Shayna?"

Harlow shook her head. "She's working at the medical center tonight."

Shayna worked admissions in the emergency department and

had helped get Harlow's sister a similar position as receptionist at the main desk.

They drove down her street to Main Street and made a right. Main Street turned into County Road 13. Trees lined the sides, and Harlow occasionally caught the glimpse of a shifter or some wild animal as the light reflected off its eyes.

"So what do you think got into our grandmothers?" Harlow asked, turning down the volume on the radio.

"Honestly, I don't know. Gram is convinced that I can choose to not be gay, and she thinks it's a phase. But an arranged marriage? That's a whole new level of crazy."

"Right?" Harlow twisted in her seat to face Curtis. "How archaic is that? And Grandma was so blasé about it, like she thought I'd just fall in line. No offense, but I'm not marrying you."

Curtis snorted and laughed. "You're such a mean witch!"

She swatted his leg before flipping him off.

A few seconds later, Curtis pulled into a parking lot nearly hidden behind the trees. The lot was almost full, but he found a spot big enough for his Tahoe and parked. Harlow stepped down, grateful she was wearing boots. Had she still been wearing her strappy heels, her toes would have frozen. She grabbed a black wool knit wrap that she had brought along as an afterthought and was glad she did as a cold wind ripped through the trees.

Adjacent to the parking lot was a gondola lift station for the gondolas that ran up the side of Miles Mountain. A large man in a black suit stood outside the station like a sentry, checking the IDs of a man and woman. As Harlow drew closer, she noticed he had an earpiece.

Tugging her wrap tighter around her shoulders, Harlow stepped up to the guard, following Curtis's lead.

"Driver's licenses."

Heeding his request, they handed their IDs over. After he

looked at each one to verify they were legal, he nodded at them and stepped to the side, letting them pass through to inside the station, where there was yet another guard manning the lift.

From the outside, the gondola looked like standard issue: metal on the bottom half and all windows for the top half. On the inside, it was anything but standard. The windows were blacked out, and each wall was lined with a plush bench. Soft lighting created a dreamy vibe. The man and the woman who had gone in right before them were the only other people in the car. They were too busy kissing to notice they had company. Harlow and Curtis chose a bench as far away as possible and waited. The wait wasn't very long before the door clanged shut and the gondola jerked as it began its ascent up the mountain.

Harlow couldn't help but watch the couple as their kissing progressed to a level ten PDA. The woman, wearing a black dress much shorter than Harlow's, so basically a shirt, was pressed against her lover with one leg thrown over his lap. He was gripping her ass tight. She rocked against him, her left hand buried in his hair as they kissed. Harlow watched, fascinated, as the man's hand slipped underneath the woman's dress. A gasp and a moan later made Harlow flush, and she looked away while adjusting her skirt so it covered more of her thighs, which she had pressed together, hoping to relieve her sudden arousal.

It seemed like the gondola was going at a snail's pace, and Harlow was glad when it finally came to a stop. There was a loud clank, and a vibration shuddered through the lift when it was locked into place at the station. The couple managed to separate and left with their arms around each other.

"If this ride had been any longer, they'd have had to send in a clean-up crew. Those two were really into each other," Harlow commented with a laugh.

"Yeah, no shit. There was no shame in their game." Curtis fanned his face with a hand. "It was kind of hot."

A narrow passageway lit by white twinkle lights led to a huge metal door that was blanketed with protective runes and glyphs. Mounted above the door was a neon sign that displayed one word: *Silk*. They had finally arrived.

Two bouncers stood on each side of the door. They wore sunglasses even though it was nighttime. Harlow only knew of one species who did this: hellhounds. Flames of hellfire burned in their eyes, and making eye contact could be fatal.

After verifying their identification again, one of the bouncers grabbed the door handle. As soon as the door opened, the heavy electronic drum and bass beat of house music poured forth.

Silk wasn't an ordinary nightclub and sure beat out anything the Haven Saloon or the Dirty Knuckle had to offer. Stepping through the door was like stepping through a portal to a new world. Silk's hellhound owner, Melaina Savage, added a little bit of underworld flavor to the décor of the club, which was a series of connected caves.

"Each room has its own theme. Here is the main nightclub." Curtis shouted his explanation over the music. "There are various levels. We can stay here or go to the supernatural room. Your choice."

"Let's stay here," she shouted back. Instinctually her hips swayed with the beat as they walked to a crowded bar for drinks. With gin and tonic in hand, Harlow grabbed Curtis and started pulling him toward the dance floor when she came to a sudden stop. Curtis practically knocked her over, and some of her drink spilled onto her hand. Straight ahead, watching over the dance floor, was Ryker. He stood at an angle, so she could see his profile. His hair was pulled back in a man bun and the scruff he was sporting earlier in the week had been shaved off. A glimpse of a tattoo peeked up above the collar of his black dress shirt, which was tucked into black jeans. The chain from his wallet caught the light and drew her attention to his ass. Damn.

"Who is tall, dark, and dangerous that you're eye fucking?" Curtis said in her ear, snapping her out of her daze. She wouldn't be surprised if she had drool hanging off her lip.

"That's the guy I stopped Amanda from hitting the other day."

"Damn, girl. He stops traffic for sure."

Harlow laughed at her friend and took a deep breath to get her wits about her. "Come on."

She grabbed Curtis's hand again, and they continued on to the dance floor.

"Who knew my fiancée was so bossy," Curtis said just as they passed Ryker. Harlow didn't see her friend wink at the biker.

"We're not getting married!" she yelled over her shoulder. "But we are dancing!"

Curtis was a great dancer, and they moved together to the music. He was safe. Harlow didn't have to worry about him getting aroused and grinding an erection into her like some guys did at clubs. She didn't have to worry about Curtis slipping something into her drink. She could just let go and have fun, forgetting about her grandmother's ridiculous expectations.

As Harlow danced, she couldn't stop looking at Ryker. Between his stance and hulking figure, he reminded her of a gargoyle watching over the sea of people. He wasn't watching everyone, though. His gaze was fixed on her. The longer he watched her, the more it turned her on. Her movements became more seductive and suggestive. A slow roll of her hips, an arch of her back. All for him. Harlow imagined Ryker dancing with her, his big hands moving over her body, cupping her breasts from behind before running a hand up her thigh and under her dress. He'd slide her panties to the side or rip them off completely, and slip a finger inside her. Harlow closed her eyes and bit her lip, imagining losing control. Hands on her hips gripped hard enough to stop her movements, and she glanced over her shoulder to see Curtis. His eyes were narrowed into slits, and he was frowning. Her gaze darted over to Ryker, and she saw he was still watching her, his nostrils flared. He flicked a tongue across his bottom lip, his mouth curled up in a knowing smirk. Oh goddess, he probably smelled her arousal. Was he like Elsmed—could he read her thoughts?

"Harlow, what was that?" Curtis asked before dropping his hands from her hips and taking a step back, putting space between them.

"What was what?"

"You were practically dry humping me."

"Sorry. I must have been caught up in the music." She tipped her glass up and drew an ice cube into her mouth. The back of her neck was sweaty, her hair damp, and arousal pulsed through her body like an electrical charge. "I need some air."

"Well, we're in a cave so that's kind of hard. Come on, let's take a break." She followed Curtis through the crowd of people packed onto the dance floor, and she hid her face behind her hair, avoiding looking at Ryker when they walked by. She could have sworn she heard a low growl. The sound elicited a wave of goose bumps and caused her nipples to harden. It took every ounce of willpower to keep moving past him.

Curtis found two seats at the bar and ordered another round of drinks. After looking at Harlow, he ordered her a glass of water too. He peeled his suit jacket off and rolled up the sleeves of his dress shirt, revealing a tattoo on the inside of his forearm. It was the triple moon symbol, a circle with a half-moon on either side facing away, like reverse parentheses. The symbol was an ancient one that represented the three phases of the moon: waxing crescent, full, and waning crescent. It was also commonly believed to represent the triple goddess: maiden, mother, and crone. Curtis had added his own flair by incorporating rainbow colors into the simple design.

"Are you ready for some real talk?" Curtis asked, as soon as the bartender had set their drinks down and walked away.

"Maybe."

"You need to get laid. You broke up with what's his face douche canoe back in March, and it's been drier than the Sahara for you ever since. I think that biker dude is the perfect opportunity. Have one night of ridiculously sinful, dirty sex."

Harlow scowled around the straw at the mention of her ex-boyfriend. Fortunately, he didn't live in Havenwood Falls anymore, so she didn't have to see his lying, cheating face. She finished taking a sip before responding. "You know I don't do one-night stands."

"Bah." Curtis waved her off. "You've been trying to be a good little Augustine for far too long. It's time to live a little. Oh!" His face lit up like he just won the lottery. "Even better. Don't make it a one-night stand. Go on a few dates with him and take him for a spin. It's time to get back on the horse. If you know what I mean?" He wiggled his eyebrows.

"You're being fucking ridiculous." She said this with a laugh, though, entertained by her friend's antics. "Why would I do this?"

"Well, for one, he's hot and you have an itch that needs to be scratched. Two, I see the way he looks at you and you look at him —smolder, baby. The attraction is mutual, so it's not like you're going in for dental surgery or anything. Three, and the best of all, is that it would piss your grandmother off. Teach Mathilde to try to control who you marry. An Augustine dating a member of SIN? Harlow, honey, you'll be the talk of the town."

It had to have been the alcohol clouding her brain, because

Harlow was actually considering it. Curtis's plan had merit, and he was right about all three points. But could she go through with it and use Ryker like that? She adjusted herself on the stool and crossed her legs. The sight of her boots reminded her of the reason why she bought them in the first place: her fantasy about riding behind Ryker on his bike and being pressed up close against him, his hips cradled between her thighs.

"Fuck it. Okay, let's do this. How do I do this?"

Curtis actually squealed and tapped his hands against the bar like a drum. "Another round," he yelled down to the bartender who was at the opposite end, and pointed at their empty glasses. "Oh, and shots—Death by Sex!"

This got a few catcalls and laughs from everyone else at the bar —a few looks, too.

Harlow groaned and shook her head. "I hope I don't regret this, Parker!"

Two hours later, Harlow had lost count of how many drinks Curtis had ordered. She had also lost sensation in a lot of places and was feeling blissfully numb. Curtis's phone lit up from where it was set on the bar. He snatched it up and grinned.

"Part-time lover has finally arrived, and he's waiting for me in his kink room," he announced.

"His wh-what?" she sputtered, unsure she heard him correctly.

"You heard me. I'm not sure how long we'll be. If you don't hear from me, are you good to call Luber for a ride or someone else?" He tilted his head in Ryker's direction and stood up, placing a hundred-dollar bill on the bar. "Tell me how Operation Get Some goes."

He winked at her and before she could say or do anything, he disappeared into the crowd.

A half hour later, Harlow finished the drink she had been nursing. She hadn't heard from Curtis, so she sent him a text.

Minutes later, the text showed as unable to deliver. After several attempts, she gave up, silently cursing the shitty cell service in town. She was about ready to call Luber when Ryker appeared next to her. With his elbows on the bar, he leaned forward when the bartender approached.

"Hey, Crusher, whatcha want?" he asked.

"Bourbon. Make it a double." His voice rumbled and resonated through Harlow. She pretended to ignore he was so close to her while hyperaware of his presence. How could she not be? He was huge, easily a foot taller than her, and his muscles bulged, testing the very fabric of his shirt. His scent swirled around her. It reminded her of cedar and winter air when it was laden with snow and wood smoke. She could sense him looking at her, so she slowly turned her head to return the stare. Up close and with his hair pulled away from his face, his gorgeous dark blue eyes, ringed with thick dark eyelashes, were on full display. His nose was slightly crooked, like it had been broken before and didn't heal properly. Being clean shaven revealed his square jawline and the true thickness of his neck. "Where's your fiancé, Country Club? He's been gone a long time."

"Who? Oh, you mean Curtis? He's not my fiancé. Well, my grandmother wanted him to be, but he's gay and I'm not into him that way. At all. My grandmother can be a little overbearing. You know how family can be. Am I right?" *Oh, sweet Jesus, I'm babbling!* Harlow cringed internally at the verbal vomit she just threw up. *Damn the booze!*

"Don't know about the family part, but I am glad to hear he's not your fiancé. Any man who would leave you alone this long, looking as good as you do, doesn't deserve you."

"Oh. Thank you." Harlow smiled and sat up straighter, preening at his compliment.

"Can I get you another drink?"

"Actually, I was going to call Luber. Curtis was my ride, but I don't think he's coming back. He was meeting someone in a kink room? I don't even want to know what goes on there." She shuddered, and Ryker laughed.

"He'll probably be a while. Tell you what, have a drink with me, and I'll take you home. I owe you, since you saved my ass."

Harlow regarded him. This was the moment she could initiate Operation Get Some. He'd take her home, and she'd invite him inside, in more ways than one. Before she could talk herself out of saying yes, she agreed. Ryker smiled and ordered her a gin and tonic.

"How did you know that's what I was drinking?" she asked, surprised.

Ryker pointed at his nose. "I'm a lion shifter and have an enhanced sense of smell. I could smell the quinine in the tonic water and juniper gives gin a distinct scent."

"Wow! Impressive. Now, let's back things up. The bartender called you Crusher. What's that all about?"

After taking a long pull of bourbon, Ryker turned toward Harlow, keeping one elbow on the bar. "That's my road name for the club."

"Why? Do you crush a lot of hearts?" she teased.

He paused and regarded her before answering. "More like bones."

Silence hung in the air between them as she processed that information. Based on his size alone, she imagined breaking bones came easy. He could probably snap her arm like a twig. She didn't get any warning vibes from him, though. He came across as more protective. Like he would hurt anyone who tried to harm her.

"That's honest."

He shrugged. "The punishment usually fits the crime."

They finished their drinks, and when Harlow stood up, she swayed and almost fell over.

"Whoa, easy there, Country Club. I got you." Ryker wrapped his arm around her waist and waved to the bartender. The crowd parted for him as he guided them to the entrance. A bouncer nodded at Ryker and opened the door.

A gust of arctic wind blasted them as soon as they stepped outside, and Harlow shivered, her wrap providing little warmth. Inside, the club was almost tropical from the number of sweaty bodies. Ryker seemed unfazed by the change in temperature. He noticed her shivering and drew her closer to his side.

"One of the perks of being a lion shifter," he whispered in her ear. "I run at a hotter temperature. Stick close to me, and I'll keep you warm."

Ryker wasn't lying. He radiated warmth, and she wrapped her arms around his waist, clinging to him like a barnacle.

"Mmm . . . you are warm. And you smell good." She inhaled his winter forest scent deeply and then froze, horrified at what she had just done. She buried her face, out of sheer mortification, in his chest, which rumbled when he laughed.

The gondola to take them down to the parking lot was packed, and they had to stand. Ryker kept her steady—she might as well have been holding onto a steel beam. He was as unaffected by the swaying of the gondola as he was the temperature. Harlow focused on keeping her mouth shut before the alcohol made her say anything else remotely idiotic, like how she wanted to climb him like a tree.

The gondola docked, and they filed out with the other passengers. Ryker kept his arm around Harlow's shoulders as they walked across the parking lot to the back corner on the left, where he stopped next to his bike. It was a Harley Davidson, and the black paint almost blended in with the night.

"Have you ever ridden a motorcycle before?" he asked her.

"No."

He nodded and bent over to unlatch a bag on the back. He pulled out a helmet and hoodie. "Put these on."

Harlow set her wrap down on the narrow back seat and pulled the hoodie on. She was practically swimming in it, and it covered more than her dress did, but it was warm and smelled like Ryker. She wondered if he'd let her keep it. Next, she put the helmet on and struggled with the buckle. Ryker chuckled and stepped in front of her, taking the two straps into his hands. She tilted her head up toward him so he wouldn't have to bend over as far. Even in her high heels, the height difference was significant. Ryker gently brushed some stray hairs aside and free of the strap running underneath her chin. His hands were rough on her skin, but she liked the sensation and leaned into his touch. She watched his face as he made some final adjustments, noticing when his gaze drifted to her lips.

Just when she thought he was going to kiss her, Ryker stepped away and pulled his leather vest out of the compartment on the other side. He stuffed her wrap in and latched the compartment closed. He straddled his bike and gestured for Harlow to climb on board. She walked around to the left side of the bike as directed and followed his instructions, placing her left foot on a peg and using his shoulders for support, then swinging her right leg over to the other side. The leather was cold against her ass, and her teeth immediately started chattering.

"Scooch forward closer to me. I'll keep you warm. It's going to get colder once we start moving."

"Well, winter is coming." It was a popular line from one of her favorite shows, and if the opportunity presented itself to use it, she took full advantage.

"You watch *Game of Thrones?*" he asked, turning to look at her over his shoulder.

"Yes. Do you?"

"It's one of my favorite shows."

"Me too." The idea that they had something in common helped Harlow to relax. Their attraction to each other was obvious, but knowing there could be more than just lust didn't make her plan to use Ryker seem as shallow. She wouldn't have to pretend so hard.

"Okay, so hold onto me and lean with me when I go around corners and curves. I can't have you moving around back there, as it's harder to steer the bike. Got it?"

"Got it."

Using his body, Ryker centered the bike and raised the kickstand with his left foot. With just that little movement, Harlow moved closer, squeezing her legs around his body. Leaning forward, she wrapped her arms around his waist, pressing her boobs against his back patch.

He turned the key and fired up the engine, which made her entire body vibrate. *Thank Goddess I don't have to pee*, she thought.

Then they were off, and Harlow squealed, gripping Ryker tighter. Closing her eyes, she buried her face in his back. After a few minutes, she relaxed and opened her eyes, sitting up a little straighter to look around. The wind rushed past her face, reminding her of downhill skiing. The mountain air always smelled the freshest when she was flying downhill at a ridiculous speed. Here, the air combined with Ryker's scent, and she wished she could bottle it. Free of the confines of a car, the entire universe stretched out before her. Gobsmacked, she tilted her head back to take in the expanse of stars. They were in a waxing gibbous moon period, and the almost full orb seemed to hover over the town, making snowcapped peaks glow against the dark night sky. The natural beauty of Havenwood Falls never ceased to amaze her, but with it on display like this, while pressed against a man who made her pulse race, Harlow was left breathless. Ryker draped his arm over her left leg and began to lightly caress her calf, which she barely felt through her boot, but it was enough to know he was touching her in such a way. Between that subtle touch and the vibration of the bike, Harlow thought her panties were going to melt right off. If it was possible to spontaneously combust from sensory overload, she was rapidly approaching that point.

Before she knew it, Ryker was pulling up in front of her house. He cut the engine, restoring quiet to her neighborhood.

"Wait, how do you know where I live?" she asked, realizing she had never told him.

"I asked around about you."

"You did? Stalk much?"

This caused Ryker to laugh as he helped her to dismount. "I'm a lion. It's what I do."

"Fair point, stalker," she said with a wink and handed him his helmet.

She was still unsteady on her feet, a combination of the motorcycle ride and the alcohol. Ryker walked her to her door. Before she unlocked it, she turned and stepped closer to him—so close she could feel the warmth radiating off of his body.

"Do you want to come inside?" she asked, looking up at him and drawing her lower lip in between her teeth, trying to look as seductive as possible.

Ryker placed his hands on her hips and leaned forward so his forehead was pressed against hers. Reaching up, she threaded her fingers through his hair. With a tilt of her head, his mouth was on hers. What had been simmering embers exploded into scorching flames, and Harlow moaned, parting her lips, opening up to

Ryker. His tongue slipped inside and was even hotter than his hands that were moving up her back as he pulled her into an embrace. He tasted of bourbon, and she couldn't get enough. Suddenly, Harlow was against the door, and Ryker's hands were under her dress, cupping her bare ass, tilting her so she rubbed against his hardness. Wrapping her legs around his waist brought him closer, and she gasped with pleasure. And just like in her fantasy on the dance floor, one of Ryker's fingers moved underneath her soaked lace panties and slid inside her.

"Oh!" she cried out against his lips, and holding onto his shoulders, she rode his hand as he inserted another finger, filling her. Pressure kept building, and she cried out again when he brushed against her clit, sending her over the edge. An electric wave of warmth washed over her body, and she clung to Ryker with shaking arms and legs. Her face was buried in the crook of his neck, her breathing erratic as she came down from her peak. Ryker removed his fingers, and she slowly unwrapped her legs from his waist. Leaning against her door, grateful for a steady surface to support her, Harlow looked up at Ryker. "Shall we take this inside?"

He brought his fingers to his mouth and she watched as he slowly sucked the two that had been inside her clean, like he was savoring her flavor. It was quite possibly the most erotic thing Harlow had ever seen.

"No, that was a taste of what's to come. You're still drunk. When I have you—and I will have you—I want you to be sober so you remember everything. Feel everything," he said with a growl, and placing a hand at the curve of her waist, he pulled Harlow forward, capturing her mouth with his. This time it wasn't bourbon she tasted, but her own essence. Ryker sucked on her bottom lip and released it with a pop. "See you soon, Country

Club," he said, before walking away and leaving her a trembling hot mess of hormones on the front porch.

Good Goddess, I am so out of my league.

CHAPTER 3

*T*he next morning, Harlow woke with a pounding headache and hazy memories of the night before. Her cheeks burned with mortification when she remembered what had transpired on her front porch for all the neighbors to see. With the porch light on, she might as well have been on a stage. But her lips still ached from their kiss, a delicious ache and a reminder of Ryker's promise. In the bright light of day, her plans for Operation Get Some seemed foolish, but now that she had a taste, she was bound and determined to follow through. Ryker appeared to be a willing and very much able partner.

Rolling from her side to her back, she stretched her legs, wiggling her toes underneath her white down comforter. Her feet were a little sore from breaking in her new boots. *So worth it*, she thought, smiling and replaying the previous night over in her mind.

A chime rang from somewhere in the house. Recognizing the sound as a low battery notification for her phone, Harlow climbed out of bed. Her hardwood floors were cold, and the house held a chill that meant her heat would need to be turned on soon. Once the mountains were capped with snow, it didn't take long for the rest of the box canyon to catch up. She stopped in the bathroom before going in search of her phone. It was in her clutch handbag on the small table by the front door.

Mamoru was nowhere to be found, so Harlow peeked her head out the back kitchen window and saw his white fluff. He had found a patch of sunlight and was chewing on some grass. Harlow put a cup of rabbit food in his bowl and got him some fresh water. After plugging her phone in to charge, Harlow set about making a tonic to cure her hangover.

She set a tea infuser down next to the stove and turned on her copper teakettle. Her herb cabinet was to the right of the stove, and she pulled out chamomile and turmeric. A pinch of each went into the infuser. From her refrigerator, she grabbed fresh ginger and a sprig of mint. A few shavings of ginger and two leaves of mint went into the infuser before she snapped it closed and dropped it in her favorite mug. It had a picture of Tyrion from *Game of Thrones* and said *I drink and I know things.* She had a wineglass to match. The teakettle started to whistle and steam billowed out the spout. She poured boiling water into her mug and breathed in the aroma as the herbs steeped. Just before she removed the infuser, she whispered an incantation that caused the water in her mug to come to a rapid boil. Almost as quickly as the bubbles erupted, they dissipated. Her cure was ready.

Sitting at the bistro table by the back window, Harlow took a few sips of her tea and immediately felt better. Her head stopped pounding, and the queasiness went away.

"Blessed be," she sighed.

A different kind of headache began to form when she started going through all of the missed messages from her family.

First, they were sorry, then they were concerned because she wasn't responding, and then they started taking a different tone.

The one voicemail from her grandmother telling her she was being selfish and that every Augustine has made sacrifices for the greater good really pissed her off. She fired off a group text that included her grandmother and her parents.

Harlow: No need to be concerned. I'm safe. Not happy about what happened. I'll marry who I love when I meet the right person.

The responses started immediately, and Harlow felt a stab of guilt. They probably were genuinely worried about her.

Mom: I agree with you, honey. Call me.

Dad: Glad you're safe, sweet pea.

G-Ma: We'll talk.

Having checked in, Harlow left her phone to finish charging. Walking into her bedroom, she snapped her fingers, and her bed started to make itself à la Mary Poppins. She pointed at her closet and selected a pair of black leggings and an emerald-green long-sleeved T-shirt. They floated through the air and landed on her bed. Fortunately, she wasn't restricted from using a little bit of magic in her own home. Crossing the room to her dresser, she picked out underwear and a bra.

After taking a quick shower and blow-drying her hair, she got dressed. As she was getting ready to leave to meet Shayna, she went to grab her fleece pullover from the coatrack when she spotted Ryker's hoodie. Being surrounded by his scent was too much to resist, so she pulled it on and slipped out the door.

Sakura Buffet was located two blocks from her house, so she walked, enjoying the crisp fall day. Halloween decorations were on full display, and she chuckled at the human houses because their ideas of witches, vampires, and ghosts were way off. Most of the humans in Havenwood Falls had no idea they lived among the real deal.

Harlow spotted Shayna sitting in one of the booths by the

window when she first stepped inside the restaurant. She was bent over a menu, her brown hair partially hiding her face. Several of the tables in the dining area were already full, even though Sakura had just opened. Sometimes, like at Coffee Haven, there was a line waiting for the doors to open.

Shayna looked up when Harlow approached, and her eyebrows rose. She paused with her glass of water halfway to her mouth.

"What are you wearing?" she asked. "Biker chick is a new look for you."

Harlow looked down at the black hoodie. She hadn't really paid attention, and it was dark when she received it. A ghost of Uncle Sam riding a motorcycle with a ghost of a buffalo running along beside him was screen-printed on the front, along with a logo for the 77th Annual Sturgis Bike Week. "Oh, this? There's a story behind this."

She sat down across from her friend.

"I hope it's a good one. I need a break from work talk and school talk. Midterms have fried my brain." In addition to working part time at the medical center and at Burger Bar, Shayna was taking online college courses.

Over plates piled high with fried rice, General Tso's chicken, tempura, and beef and broccoli, Harlow filled Shayna in on the past twenty-four hours. She had to edit the supernatural parts out since Shayna was human and had no idea Harlow was a descendant of a long line of witches.

Shayna threw her head back and laughed out loud when Harlow told her about Operation Get Some. Several diners looked over in their direction after her outburst. "So after Curtis left me at Silk, Ryker gave me a ride home and loaned me this sweatshirt."

"And that's it?" Shayna asked, frowning with disappointment.

"No, there's more." Harlow leaned forward and gestured for

Shayna to as well. "We kissed, and then he finger-banged me on my front porch," she whispered.

Shayna's mouth dropped open.

"What?" She laughed and shook her head, her brown eyes twinkling with amusement. "You go, Harlow! That's way more exciting than my Saturday night. I swear, the week leading up to the full moon makes people nuts. The ER is always busiest this time of the month. Ugh, and you know how I don't like all that gross medical shit? Well, this guy came in, dripping blood all over the floor, and I swear he was holding his arm on. I almost lost it right there." Shayna pressed a hand against her stomach and shuddered.

"I bet." Harlow often wondered why her friend, whose stomach went queasy at the sight of blood, worked at the medical center.

They chatted some more and finished eating lunch.

"So are you going to go out with him again to follow through with this plan Curtis cooked up?" Shayna asked as they were getting ready to leave.

"My hormones might go on strike if I don't."

Three days later her hormones were on strike. Harlow's dreams had been hijacked by Ryker, and she'd taken to sleeping in his hoodie so she could be surrounded by his scent. The damn biker had given her a taste, and now that's all her body craved. He hadn't called, but they had never exchanged numbers. As Harlow was closing down Coffee Haven for the day, she contemplated going next door to Callie's to see if she could get Ryker's number from Ronan.

Harlow gathered up the trash and went out the side door to the alley. When she was lifting up the lid for the dumpster, she heard a motorcycle. The rumble of the pipes echoed off the brick walls. She tossed the trash bag in and when she turned to go back inside, saw the source of the noise. Ryker sat on his bike at the end of the alley with the engine idling, which he turned off when Harlow approached.

"I was just thinking about you," she said, scanning him from head to toe. Damn, he was hot, she thought. His dark jeans hugged muscular thighs, and despite the cold, he wore a white T-shirt underneath his leather vest. The late-day sunlight filtered through the trees that lined Town Square Park and made the tattoos on his arms appear brighter. His hair was wild and free, a true lion's mane. Ryker took his sunglasses off and set them on top of the windblown tangles. They made eye contact, and her breath stuttered.

"Oh yeah, what kind of thoughts were you having?" He raised an eyebrow and licked his lips as he looked her over. The slow, predatory perusal of her body made Harlow's mouth go dry and her panties damp. It also made her feel sexy as hell even though she was wearing jeans and a sweater, which was covered by a black Coffee Haven apron. Not exactly the sexiest attire.

"Uh, um, I have your hoodie still and didn't have your number?" Harlow had never been more appreciative of her Japanese heritage than that moment, because her olive skin didn't blush easily.

"I have your sweater scarf thing. How about we arrange a trade . . . over dinner?"

"I'd like that." Harlow stepped closer and ran her hand along his bike's handlebars, which were taller than what she was used to seeing.

"Those are ape hangers," Ryker explained. "They work better with my height than the standard issue."

"Oh. I don't know anything about bikes."

"I know. I like that about you. So, dinner. What's your schedule like—are you free Friday night?"

He tugged on Harlow's apron strings and pulled her closer until she was straddling his thigh. It took all her willpower to not sink down and grind. She placed a hand on his chest to keep herself from falling against him, but when he wrapped an arm around her waist, she slid her hand up and around the back of his neck, underneath his thick hair. With Ryker sitting down, their height was almost even. He angled his head just right, an invitation she accepted by placing her lips on his. Just like before, it was as if electricity were coursing through her veins, a pleasant buzz that caused her nipples to harden. Ryker's tongue teased along the seam of her lips, and she opened for him. Their kiss deepened, and Harlow's legs became weak. She sank down on Ryker's thigh and moaned in his mouth when the seam of her jeans pressed against her sensitive clit.

"Harlow Augustine!" The shout was as effective as being doused by freezing water from the falls in the middle of January. Harlow broke off the kiss, turning around to see her grandmother standing less than five feet away.

"Fuck," Harlow muttered. Her legs were unsteady when she climbed off of Ryker's thigh. "I have to go."

"I guess so, and it's a damn shame." Ryker flashed a lopsided grin. "We didn't finalize dinner. Are you free Friday?"

Harlow ran through her schedule in her head. She had to work Saturday night at the Country Club, as they were having a Halloween party for the members. Friday night was free. "I'm available."

"Good. I'll pick you up at seven o'clock." He put his sunglasses back on, fired up his bike, and pulled out onto Main Street.

Harlow watched him leave before turning to face her grandmother, her arms crossed in front of her chest. "We can talk out here, or you can come inside. I have to finish closing."

"I'd prefer a more private setting instead of sharing out here for everyone to witness." Mathilde gestured at the dozen or so people walking around the Main Street businesses. Not one of them was paying any attention to Harlow and her grandmother.

"It was just a kiss, Grandma," Harlow said, walking down the alley toward the side entrance. She heard her grandmother's heels as she followed behind.

"You were practically on top of him. Certainly not ladylike behavior. And with a man like that. He's not good enough for you."

Pausing with her hand on the doorknob, Harlow closed her eyes and took a deep breath. *Goddess, give me strength.* They stepped inside, and Harlow locked the door before walking back behind the counter to unload the dishwasher, which had finished its cycle while she was outside. "We're getting to know each other, and he's a nice guy—respectful even. Besides, have you looked at him?" She fanned herself, laying it on thick.

Based on the scowl, her grandmother was not amused, but Harlow was—Operation Get Some was already having its intended effect.

"Curtis is respectful."

"Curtis is gay, or did his grandmother leave that part out when you were negotiating our marriage?"

Her grandmother pursed her lips and lowered her eyes— actually looking contrite.

"Yes, that was a misunderstanding. Your father and uncle let me have it after you left. I want to apologize for springing that on you." She pulled out a chair and sank wearily down. "Being a high priestess is exhausting sometimes. I want you more involved, Harlow. You've never shown an interest in the coven, not like Gallad or your sister. You have skills and can be an asset. Most importantly, I want you protected, and I need to know you can protect yourself. What happened to Sedona—"

She trailed off, and they both looked at the patch in the wall that connected Coffee Haven to Sedona's store, Shelf Indulgence.

Sedona was attacked, and a hole was blown through the wall. Fortunately, the store suffered more damage than Sedona—well, physical damage at least. Harlow suspected the empathic witch was haunted by memories. Sedona was like Harlow and on the fringe of coven life, resisting her aunt's influence.

"There are threats of more attacks to come." This statement hung heavy in the air, and Harlow looked at her grandmother— really looked at her. Mathilde Augustine was well over one hundred years old but usually looked a youthful sixty. Her hair was now threaded more heavily with silver. It was pinned up in a loose bun, so her face was in full view, revealing bags under her eyes, and there was a sagginess around her jawline that hadn't been there before.

"Grandma . . ." Harlow sat down across from her grandmother and captured her hand, which was cold and the skin felt papery thin.

"I won't fight you on the marriage, Harlow. I should have known you would react that way. You've always been an advocate for free will."

"Thank you. I thought you had lost it. 'It's time to put grandma in a home,' ran through my mind," she teased, and Mathilde chuckled.

"I have at least a hundred more years in me, missy." She sighed and sat up straighter. "But I won't budge on the training sessions. Those are Court ordered. Besides, I'd feel better knowing you are practiced in defense."

"Agreed. That's a decent compromise."

"Suppose you won't be willing to compromise some more and not associate with that biker?"

"Not a chance." Harlow stood up. "Can I make you a coffee to go—a Witch's Brew with that energy tincture you like?"

"That would be lovely, dear. I'm glad we talked and cleared the air."

"Me too, Grandma." Harlow leaned over and kissed her grandmother's cheek before going behind the counter to make her coffee.

They made plans for Harlow to start training every Sunday afternoon and Wednesday evening. Mathilde left a few minutes later, and Harlow finished closing up. She brought the bank bag, which contained all of the cash and credit card receipts, to Willow's office. When she opened the top drawer, a pink pacifier rolled toward the front, and Harlow smiled, discovering a treasure trove of baby items like a pair of mismatched socks, one pastel green and the other white, both with ruffle cuffs. There was a teething ring and a unicorn plushy. Willow's office was always super organized before she became a mom. Now there were piles of paper on the desk and a basket of toys in the corner that had spilled over onto the floor. A strong longing to be a mother, to carry a child in her womb, hit Harlow out of nowhere. The emotion was so powerful it practically knocked the wind out of her, and she sat down hard in the desk chair.

What the hell was that? Spooked, Harlow shoved the bank bag on top of the baby items, shut the drawer, and quickly left.

CHAPTER 4

"*Y*ou should, like, totally wear this one." Harlow's sister, Taylor, held up a black V-neck cashmere sweater from where she was standing in the walk-in closet. "Wear this with your dark denim jeans and those kick-ass boots, which I'm going to be borrowing. Soon."

"Over my cold dead body you're borrowing these. I'll never see them again."

"Won't be the first witch sister in history to die over a pair of shoes."

Harlow rolled her eyes. Her sister never got tired of making *Wizard of Oz* jokes, which was one of their favorite movies they watched together—next to *Practical Magic*. Taylor was over helping Harlow get ready for her date with Ryker. She was anxious to meet the bad boy who had their grandmother in a state.

Taking her sister's advice, she put on the dark denim jeans and black sweater. The cashmere was soft and warm. The sweater hugged her curves, and the V-neck dipped low enough to be sexy but not inappropriate. Her favorite bra pushed up the girls and showcased them just right.

Harlow wore her hair down. The soft waves cascaded down her back. She did her makeup, accentuating the slight slant of her eye with eyeliner. She was sitting on the sofa, counting down the minutes, when there was a knock on the front door. Taylor, who was next to her texting on her phone, jumped up and raced to the door. Harlow walked up behind her as Taylor was letting Ryker in. He was so tall he had to duck to clear the doorframe. In his hands he carried a giant potted mum the color of red wine.

"Whoa," Taylor said, staring up at Ryker, apparently rendered speechless. He did look good. His long hair was combed out and smooth. A dusting of stubble lined his square jaw. He wore a black-and-gray plaid flannel shirt, the top buttons undone to accommodate his thick neck.

"Ryker, come in. This is my sister, Taylor. Is that for me?" She pointed at the plant.

"It is. I didn't know what flowers you like, and they match the trim on your house—thought the mums would look nice on your porch." He shrugged and handed her the flowers.

"That's very thoughtful. Thank you." Standing on tiptoe, she kissed his cheek.

"Did you ride your bike here? Can I see it?" Taylor asked, hands clasped in front of her like she was just shy of begging.

"No, I drove my Bronco. It's supposed to get below freezing tonight, and it can get really cold for passengers not used to riding."

"Plus, it will keep Harlow's hair from turning into a disaster," Taylor added with a grin, and Ryker laughed.

"She's gorgeous no matter what. She could be bald and will still be beautiful."

Taylor rolled her eyes, which caused Ryker to laugh some more. Harlow waved her hand and whispered a spell. Suddenly a gust of wind appeared out of nowhere and swirled around Taylor, whipping her hair, which was long like Harlow's but straighter with red highlights, into chaos.

"Hey!" she cried. "I'm going out too, you know!" With an annoyed huff, Taylor stomped down the hall to the bathroom.

"Well, that was fun," Harlow said, turning her attention back to Ryker. "Want the grand tour?"

"Sure." She pointed at Ryker's boots and explained her house rule of leaving shoes at the door. She set the mums on the coffee table and out of Mamoru's reach while Ryker took his boots off.

Hyperaware of Ryker at her back, Harlow showed him around her bungalow. She pointed to the guest bedroom to the right of the front door and across the hall from the living room. In between the guest bedroom and her bedroom was the bathroom. When they walked by, Taylor was combing her fingers through her hair. Across from the bathroom were stairs that led to the second floor.

"My meditation room is up here. Since the ceiling slopes, it wasn't really a good spot for a bedroom," she explained as they climbed the stairs. Ryker couldn't stand up straight except at the center of the room. Skylights were on each side, providing glimpses of stars. A yoga mat, blocks, and a bolster were stacked in a cubicle in the left corner. White candles, large and small, covered almost every available surface. Along the right wall there was a beanbag chair next to a bookshelf so loaded with books, the shelves were bowed. A desk was in front of the wide window that overlooked the street and Cook's Corner Park. Bundles of sage and a collection of crystals were scattered across the top. The only light was from the overhead ceiling fan, and it was a low wattage bulb. The dim lighting added warmth to the toffee-colored walls.

"Wow. It's really peaceful up here," Ryker commented. He stood with his head back and eyes closed, breathing in the positive energy.

"This is where I come to recharge."

She led him back downstairs and showed him the kitchen. With butter-yellow walls and whitewashed cabinets, this was one of her favorite rooms. Ryker examined the shelf of cookbooks on the wall next to the stove.

"Do you like to cook?" he asked.

"I do. I hope to open run my own food truck one day. Give Tacos for Daze some competition."

"Oh yeah? What kind of food?"

"Japanese fusion. You know, traditional noodle dishes with different influences. Dishes like that."

"My sister is an amazing cook." Taylor appeared in the arched entryway, her hair tamed. "I'm heading out now to meet Paisley at Burger Bar."

"Oh, she's home?" Harlow asked.

"Yeah, for the weekend."

"Tell her I said hi and that I miss working with her."

"I will." Taylor turned to face Ryker. "It was nice meeting you."

"Same here. Do you want us to drop you off on our way out?"

"Nah. It's a quick walk. Thanks, though!" She was already walking toward the front door, her voice echoing off the walls.

A strange thwap sound came from the back of the house, and Harlow watched with amusement as Mamoru came in from the backyard through the pet door and froze. His nose twitched rapidly as he sniffed the air, detecting the new presence, and Ryker did the same thing. He looked down at the hare, and the hare looked at him. They regarded each other for a few minutes. Harlow waited for her familiar to raise the alarm if he felt any kind of threat coming from Ryker. When he didn't start thumping his hind legs and instead hopped over to sniff Ryker's feet, she relaxed. Her familiar would let her know if danger was near.

"That's Mamoru. He's not a snack," she teased. When she said that, a growl from Ryker's stomach rumbled low and deep like thunder. "I mean it."

"I won't eat your pet," he assured her. "I am hungry, though. Ready to go?"

"Oh, he's not a pet. He's my familiar." Harlow tried to keep the annoyance from her tone. Mamoru had taken offense, though, as he turned around and pooped directly in front of Ryker's feet.

"What the fuck?"

Harlow burst out laughing. "He told you!"

She continued to laugh as she walked down the hall to the bathroom, returning with a wad of toilet paper to clean up the mess.

Minutes later, Ryker was holding the passenger door to his Bronco open. It was all black and the older blockier style. Harlow scrambled inside as gracefully as possible. The inside of the cab was pure, unadulterated, concentrated Ryker, and she breathed in deep, stifling a moan just as he opened the driver's side door and effortlessly hopped in.

He took her to Fallview Tavern, a restaurant with a fantastic view of the cascading waterfalls the town was named after. The water contained mystical properties that called to supernaturals, and Harlow felt the magic humming through her veins as they drew closer. The Luna Coven had several circles located near the falls.

As far as first dates went, this was one of the better ones Harlow had been on. Ryker held doors open for her, he assisted her with her chair, and their conversation flowed naturally. They were tucked away in an alcove, an intimate setting away from the noise of the bar and heavy foot traffic areas like the kitchen and bathrooms—and away from prying ears. She learned that in addition to working at Silk, he also worked for McCabe & Sons

Construction as a laborer when needed and made deliveries for CDI. Ryker was also surprisingly open with her about his past.

"I'm not big on secrets, and I'm one to tell people like it is. With me, what you see is what you get. My brothers in the MC, they are my family. I don't have any blood family—that I'm aware of. You see, my mom abandoned me when I was two, and I was raised in the system down in Tucson. That wasn't an easy life, being a kid who's bigger than every other kid his age and has a temper."

"I can't imagine it's easy for anyone." Harlow cut into her pork chop and took a bite, waiting for Ryker to continue.

"You're right—it's pretty shitty. I got out when I was sixteen."

"You were adopted?"

"No." Ryker paused and looked past Harlow's shoulder. Emotions flickered in his blue eyes as if he was watching his memories play out on a movie screen.

"What happened?" Harlow asked. Whatever the memories were, she could tell they troubled him.

Ryker leaned forward and reached for Harlow's hand that was resting on the table near her wine glass. He clasped her hand in his, dwarfing hers. Warmth seeped into her bones, which practically turned to liquid just from the simple contact. His touch wasn't sensual this time. He was reaching out to her for strength and comfort, like she was his anchor and he didn't want to be carried away by his memories.

"I shifted for the first time and freaked the fuck out. I had no idea I was a lion shifter."

"Oh, my goddess! That had to have been terrifying. Where were you when you shifted?"

Ryker got quiet and started to pull away, but Harlow wouldn't let him. She needed to know more about this mysterious man.

"I had cut school that day and thought I had gotten away with it, until I got home to my latest temporary home and Bob, my foster 'dad' was there to greet me. We fought. It was bad. I was bigger than him, meaner, and had so much anger just boiling in my blood. Our fights had never been physical, only shouting matches. That day was different. Bob shoved me. Placed his hands right here." Ryker tapped at his chest with his free hand. "Next thing I knew, pain went ripping through my body. Joints and bones made the most horrible cracking sound, like a bunch of branches being broken all at once. Then I was on all fours, and instead of shouting, I was roaring. Bob became ghost white, and he turned to run. I bet you know what instinct that triggered?"

By this point of the story, Harlow was gripping Ryker's hand tight.

"Holy shit! He became the prey. Did you kill him?" She whispered this question and looked around covertly to make sure no one was walking by and overheard.

"No. Came real fucking close, though. I don't remember the attack so much. But I remember the hot gush of his blood filling my mouth, and the taste made me feel complete. I'd never fit in anywhere and had always been this angry misfit. It wasn't until my shift that something clicked into place. For the first time, opposing forces had become one."

"What did you do?"

"I ran and kept running—mainly fueled by fear that I was going to be arrested or put down like a rabid dog. My emotions were all over the place, so much so that I couldn't figure out how to shift back. I was forced to head into the mountains. I stumbled upon a small supernatural community in the Superstition Mountains outside of Phoenix. They saw me for what I was. I mean, African lions aren't native to Arizona. Anyway, a wolf shifter taught me how to return to my human form. He lent me clothes, too. The community offered to let me stay, and I did for a while.

Long enough to learn about what I was and how to control my shift. I moved on after a few months, picking up odd jobs here and there, eventually making my way to Colorado."

"Wow! I can't even imagine. Ever since I was little, I've known I'm a witch. My family history has been drilled into me—it still is."

"Yeah, I know. A couple of my brothers are shocked you agreed to go out with me. Your family might as well be Havenwood Falls royalty. Does that make you a princess?" Ryker smirked and let go of her hand but not before gently squeezing it first. He picked up his fork and continued eating his steak that was bigger than his plate.

Harlow rolled her eyes and reached for her glass of pinot grigio. "I'm definitely not a princess."

Ryker paused to finish chewing, regarding Harlow from across the table. A candle in the middle cast shadows and light across his face. "No. You're much more."

Warmth spread out from within when he said that, and it wasn't from the wine. *You're much more, too.* She wanted to tell him, but that admission would definitely move things beyond "just a fling" territory, and Harlow felt like she was dangling on the edge of a precipice already—dangerously close to falling.

The ride back to her house after dinner was quiet—full of unspoken expectation. Ryker held her hand, steering confidently with one hand. Harlow was relaxed. The glass of wine at dinner had taken the edge off any nerves, but she wasn't drunk like the last time Ryker had taken her home. She wondered if he would accept her invitation to come inside. When Ryker parked behind her car in the driveway and turned off the engine, she twisted in her seat to face him, only to find he was facing her. Their hands were still linked, and he gently ran his thumb along the side of her hand.

"Thank you for dinner," she said, breaking the silence. "Do you want—"

Before she could finish inviting him inside, Ryker leaned forward and at the same time tugged on her hand, drawing her closer to him on the bench seat. Then his mouth was on hers, and she let him in. Their tongues moved against each other in a slow dance. Traces of dessert, a slice of devil's food cake they had shared, sweetened his kiss, and she nibbled on his bottom lip, which apparently flipped a switch. With a growl that sounded more like a purr, Ryker lifted Harlow onto his lap.

"Oh!" she cried out in surprise. "Oh." She gave him a knowing smile once she sank down onto the bulge being barely contained by his jeans. Ryker held her hips in place and ground against her center.

"Do you like that?" His voice was husky, and he thrust again.

"Yes," she gasped and leaned forward to kiss him.

Rolling her hips in a slow grind against his erection, fingers threaded through his thick hair, Harlow immersed herself in the moment. Ryker's hands slid underneath her sweater and moved up her back. Rough callouses against her bare skin made her shiver, and her nipples hardened, the lace of her bra rubbing against the tight points, adding an extra sensation. His hands moved around to the front and cupped her breasts. Arching her back, she pressed further into his touch, encouraging him to squeeze harder. He did, right before he started to lift her sweater. Breaking the kiss, she raised her arms, and he stripped the sweater completely off, unclasping her bra in seconds. Cold air hit her nipples, and when Ryker sucked one into his hot mouth, she almost came on the spot. Her fingers were still buried in his hair, and she held him close to her breasts, begging him to suck harder. With each tug on her nipple, she cried out for more.

Ryker released her nipple and made his way up to her neck,

kissing and nipping the entire way. Every time he playfully bit down on her skin, it made her clit tingle, and she ground down on him, enjoying the way he twitched and throbbed beneath her.

Reaching down between them, she ran her hand along his length before unbuttoning his jeans. Just as she was lowering the zipper, his phone started to ring.

"I'm not answering that," he groaned in her ear when she dipped her hand into his pants and wrapped it around his dick. As soon as his phone stopped ringing, it started up again. "Fuck!"

Harlow started stroking him and looked up to see he had his head tilted back. His eyes were closed, and his chest was rising and falling rapidly.

Whoever was trying to reach him called again.

"I'm sorry, babe." Ryker peered down at her. His eyes had changed from blue to gold, and they almost glowed in the dark. "I don't want you to stop, but I need to see who's calling."

Harlow removed her hand and scooted back on his lap so he had room to reach for his phone, which was in the ashtray. This was the old school type that dropped down from beneath the dash.

Ryker frowned when he looked at the phone and immediately dialed someone. Holding the phone up to his ear, he traced lazy circles around her nipples with his other hand.

"What's up?" Ryker frowned again, and his hand slid down her side, coming to a stop on her hip. "I'm on it and right around the corner, so I'll be there fast."

"What's going on?" Harlow asked when he ended the call. She started to climb off his lap, but he stopped her.

"Some of my brothers got in a fight at the Haven Saloon and need an assist." He cupped her breasts, rolling her nipples between his fingers. "I hate to leave when things were just getting interesting."

Harlow leaned into his hands, melting at his touch. He pulled her into a hug, and her sensitive tips brushed against his shirt. He nuzzled her neck, placing soft kisses right below her ear. Harlow slowly sat up, bracing herself on his broad shoulders.

"You have to go," she said and put her sweater on sans bra, which she grabbed when she climbed off his lap. When she went to open the passenger door, she noticed all of the windows were fogged up.

"I'll be seeing you again, Country Club. We have unfinished business," Ryker said right before she shut the door. This made her smile, and she skipped up her porch steps.

The next morning, Harlow strolled into Coffee Haven in a dreamlike state. The bliss from her date had yet to wear off. Willow noticed immediately and gave her a knowing smile, her turquoise eyes twinkling.

"Oh my, you are on a totally different planet right now, aren't you?"

Harlow tied an apron around her waist and pulled her hair back in a ponytail. "Something like that." She winked.

The bell above the door chimed, signaling the arrival of the first customers of the day. Biddie Half-Moon held the door open for her best friend, Irene Beckett, who was pushing a walker in front of her. They were an odd pairing. Biddie was a retired actress who had been married seven times, and Irene was a retired teacher who had only been married once. They had one thing in common, though: gossip.

"We'll catch up later," Willow said and turned to greet Irene and Biddie as they approached the counter. Irene completely ignored Willow and zeroed in on Harlow.

"How was your date last night, dear?"

"Uh, it was fine, Ms. Beckett. How did you know?"

"It's all the talk in your neighborhood, dear. A word of advice from an elder: when getting intimate, it's best to do those things behind closed doors."

Biddie Half-Moon nodded in agreement with her busybody friend and added, "Imagine how shocked I was when I was taking Chester for his last walk before bedtime and saw you in that Bronco."

Harlow's mouth hung open in shock, then embarrassment took over. "Oh my goddess!" She pulled the bottom half of her apron up to cover her face. Willow laughing at the situation didn't help. At all.

"I have to say it made me sentimental. Made me long for the days when my tits were perky. Enjoy them while they last!" Biddie chuckled and went to join Irene at a table near the window. This was one of their favorite spots because it gave the town gossips a great view of Main Street and happenings on the square. Those two didn't miss a thing, apparently.

"Did Biddie just say tits?" a stunned Harlow asked Willow, and they both burst into laughter.

The day only got weirder from there. When Harlow showed up at the Creekwood Country Club to work the Halloween party, her dad called her into his office. His office was almost as big as her house. A L-shaped desk faced the door, and to the left was a seating area consisting of a brown suede sofa, coffee table, and two high-backed chairs in a bold pattern of greens and blues. Floor-to-ceiling windows looked out onto the golf course, which was slowly becoming shrouded in darkness as the sun set. She walked in to find her dad standing by one of these windows, his back to her. He was wearing a voluminous white shirt, black pants, and black leather boots that stopped just below his knee.

"You needed to see me, Dad?"

He turned at the sound of her voice, and that's when she saw his eye patch and a sword strapped to his leg. He was dressed as a pirate. With his salt and pepper goatee, he looked the part.

"Shut the door please, sweet pea."

She did as he asked, bracing herself for whatever conversation they were about to have. Whenever he asked her to close the door, it usually meant she was either in trouble or about to be on the receiving end of a lecture. He crossed the room and sat in one of the chairs, so Harlow chose the chair next to him. He didn't waste any time getting to the point.

"Your grandmother called me this morning and gave me an earful about you. Apparently, you're dating a member of the SIN MC? Is this true?"

"We went on *a* date."

He stood up and walked over to the sideboard where a small selection of bourbons and whiskeys were lined up. He poured himself a glass and took a long sip. "I don't agree with your grandmother on arranged marriages. That shit with Curtis was just plain idiocy. But a biker? SIN isn't a group of angels. I know you know that."

"I know, but—"

"Let me finish." He sat down next to her again. "Your grandmother does have a point about marrying one of our kind."

"Who's talking about marrying Ryker? I went on one date with him. Besides, we should be able to marry who we want. You did. Mom isn't a witch, and you're happy, right?"

Her dad didn't say anything and took another drink. He leaned forward and set his glass on the table before running a hand through his dark hair that was threaded with gray. "I love your mother, but part of me marrying her was an act of rebellion. I know my mom can be overbearing, and keeping the Augustine line strong is important. She was on me like she is on you. I don't regret marrying your mom and having you and your sister, but I regret how hard it has been for your mom. Not being accepted by your grandmother has taken its toll on her, especially since her family is in Japan. Not being a witch hasn't been easy for her either. She feels excluded."

There was a knock on the door.

"Valerio, the members are beginning to arrive," someone called from the other side. Her dad stood up, signaling an end to the conversation.

"Dad, I hear you and don't worry. I'm having some fun. Besides, Ryker is a nice guy. You should know that I wouldn't tolerate anything else."

"I know, sweet pea." He bent over and kissed her cheek before walking over to the door.

"Hey, Dad?" He stopped and looked over at her. "Can you wear the pirate costume every time we have a serious talk? I kept imagining you telling me to walk the plank." She grinned at him, and he was shaking his head and chuckling when he left.

That certainly wasn't the last of her hearing from family members. The next day she arrived at her grandparents' house for a training session. Her grandfather answered the door and gave her a hug.

"She's on the warpath. Be prepared," he whispered in her ear before they separated. "I want you to know, even though your grandmother and I started out as an arranged marriage, I didn't agree with how she went about everything with Curtis. Times have changed. Kids these days are much more independent."

"Thanks, Grandpa. Where is she?"

"The office. Good luck." He sauntered off in the direction of the living room with a book tucked under his arm while Harlow went to find her grandmother.

As soon as she walked into the office, a vase came flying at her, and she froze time. Her grandmother was next to the desk, arm still in the air post-throw. Harlow grabbed hold of the vase and then started time again.

Her grandmother clucked her tongue in disappointment. "You reacted without thinking. What would have been a better approach?"

"Other than getting hit in the head with a vase?" Harlow crossed the room and set the vase down on the table. With her hands on her hips, she squared off with her grandmother. "What if that had hit me?"

"Psshht." Mathilde waved her hand dismissively. "I would patch you up with a healing spell or tincture. An alternative response to this situation is to freeze the object or redirect it. Redirecting is better because it's less obvious to human eyes. However, if there are humans around, the best choice is to not react at all and take the hit. Learning not to respond, like not sending a man flying across a crowded bar, is what we're going to be working on today. After the lesson, we're going to talk about your recent date and behavior that is very unbecoming of an Augustine."

Goddess, give me strength.

CHAPTER 5

*M*ore than a week had passed since Ryker had taken Harlow out, and she hadn't heard from him. Then again, they hadn't exchanged phone numbers. His hoodie still hung on her coat rack, and he still had her wrap. They had been too wrapped up in each other to even think about the swap, which was the impetus for Ryker asking her out. He was never far from her thoughts. It was more than just the sex-filled dreams that had her thinking about him, but the man himself.

Ryker had shared a lot with her over dinner. He had overcome many obstacles in life. Her initial impression of him had been that he was hot but an ass. The few interactions she had with him since then changed her mind. The time they spent learning about each other also caused her to think twice about using him. If they ever went out again, she'd have to decide to end things or to go all in. Both options terrified her.

"When did things get so complicated?" she asked Shayna when they caught up over a wine tasting at Soothing Sips, a business owned by the Blackstone family, who also owned Stone Falls Winery. Brock Blackstone brought over two flights, and he couldn't keep his eyes off of Shayna. *Interesting. Once I get my shit together maybe I can do some matchmaking of my own.*

"Do you actually have feelings for Ryker?"

Harlow sighed and sipped the red blend. "I do, but I haven't heard from him, and we're so different. Maybe it's not meant to be."

"Bullshit." Shayna fished around in her bag and pulled out her cell phone.

"Who are you texting?"

"Curtis."

"Why?"

"He can get anyone's number, and I just asked him to track down Ryker's. If you like this guy, and I know you do, then you call him. Don't wait for him to call you. We're modern women, and that's how we roll."

So that's how Harlow ended up going out with Ryker two weeks later. He had been out of town on club business, which was why he hadn't contacted her. He had been planning to get in touch when he got back. She beat him to it.

Their second date was the complete opposite of their first.

"I'm showing you my world tonight, Country Club," Ryker announced when he met her in the parking lot of the SIN clubhouse. She parked next to a row of motorcycles, careful to leave plenty of space. They were having a party, and from the sounds of things, it was already in full swing. "Some pointers before we go in. Stay by me so the guys know you're mine. They don't know you and might mistake you for a club bunny."

"A what?"

"Club bunnies are chicks that hang out around the MC with aspirations to become a member's old lady. They'll literally do anything, fuck anyone to earn that title. You are nothing like them."

"Okay." Harlow swallowed hard, processing that information. "There will be skanks. Got it."

"You're going to see some crazy shit. Sex out in the open, women running around half naked, and a lot of booze. This clubhouse is way different than the country club."

"Says you. You haven't been to the Christmas party."

Ryker cocked his head and looked at her with his eyes slightly narrowed, like he was trying to figure out if she was serious. She kept a straight face and let him ponder.

"Finally, if at any time you want to leave, say the word. These parties can get out of hand. I need to keep an eye on the prospects and on you. Just watch your back, especially wearing that dress. You look incredible, by the way."

Harlow wore a leather jacket over a formfitting black V-neck dress with red suede ankle boots. The V was too deep to wear a bra, and with the way Ryker's nostrils flared when he zeroed in on her breasts, she knew he noticed. He pulled her into his arms and kissed her. He tasted of mint toothpaste, and he hadn't shaved in a few days. His stubble had already grown past the rough, bristly stage.

"Oh, and one other thing," he said, threading his fingers through hers as they started walking toward the entrance to the clubhouse. "This place is warded. If you need to use your magic, you can without getting in trouble with the Court."

"Good to know."

Ryker held the door open for her, and she stepped into chaos. His hand on the small of her back added the little bit of reassurance she needed to move forward. He hadn't been lying. The party was the living definition of debauchery. Five Finger Death Punch blasted from speakers mounted in all corners of the room, which was an open area somewhat larger than a spacious living room. A haze of cigarette and pot smoke clouded the air,

making her eyes burn. The smells of sweat, sex, and booze were also part of the mix. In the center of the room was a pool table that, aside from the bar, was the hub of activity. Bikers wearing their leather cuts indicating they were members of SIN filled the room, which reminded Harlow of a tavern. The hardwood floors were beat to hell, and neon signs for various beers decorated the walls. A few sofas were scattered throughout. A SIN member sat on one of the sofas, with a woman on her knees in front of him, sucking his dick for everyone to see. In fact, a few men watched. Around the pool table there were several high-top tables with red-cushioned, metal-back chairs. Ryker guided her toward one that was unoccupied, stopping to bro hug several guys along the way.

"Do you want a drink?" he asked as soon as she was seated.

"Sure."

"Beer or hard stuff? We don't have wine."

"That's fine. Can I get a gin and tonic?"

He nodded and headed toward the bar. Harlow observed that everyone moved out of his way. She also noticed a couple women glaring at her. They could have been twins. They looked like they spent too much time in a tanning bed and lived on diet pills, basically leathery and skinny like pieces of beef jerky. She was willing to bet money that they were club bunnies. *Back off, bunnies. He's mine.*

Ryker returned with her drink and a bourbon for him. He wasn't alone.

"Harlow, this is Savage, my VP." He introduced her to a man she knew of but had never officially met. Savage had long dark hair that turned lighter at the ends, and he was just as big as Ryker. He wore sunglasses, so it was hard to get a read on him.

"Savage, this is my girl, Harlow."

Savage's face may not have moved much to betray his reaction, but she saw his eyebrows rise above his sunglasses.

"You're Luna Coven," he stated.

"That's right."

He nodded once. "What you see here, stays here. Got it?"

"I understand."

"Good." With that he clapped Ryker on the shoulder and left. A couple more of Ryker's brothers stopped by the table, and he introduced her to them. There was Monte or "Axle" and "Trapper" or Hunter; they went by both. Hunter had a woman with him who was new to town. Izzie was her name, and she moved with the fluid grace of a dancer. The prospect, which was how Ryker referred to him, she knew as Kai because he had graduated high school the same year as Taylor and Paisley. He came into Coffee Haven often. That night, as part of his prospect duties, he was in charge of refilling their drinks and bussing tables.

"He looks up to you," Harlow commented after Kai left to get them another round. "I can tell he wants to please you. It's not out of fear but respect."

Ryker flashed a lopsided grin. "Yeah, the kid has potential. Like me, he spent some time homeless and on the streets. Unlike me, he was adopted, but apparently it wasn't a good situation. We both found a family here with the MC. If I do right by him, he'll do right for the club. I still like to scare the piss out of him every once in a while. Keeps the young ones from getting too cocky."

As the night wore on, inhibitions ceased to exist. Harlow took it all in. Women straddled bikers, letting them do whatever they wanted to their naked bodies. Some of the women played with each other, putting on a show. Harlow stiffened when the beef jerky twins approached Ryker, pressing against him, one on each side. Insecurities surfaced when she was reminded of how easily her ex had strayed. *This is just a fling. He's not your boyfriend*, she reminded herself. She did feel some satisfaction when Ryker shooed them away like they were flies trying to land on his food.

His focus remained solely on Harlow, and as things escalated around them, his hand moved farther up her thigh, slipping under her dress. She uncrossed her legs, and his eyes flashed gold at the subtle invitation.

Leaning forward, he whispered huskily in her ear over the deafening music, his breath hot against her neck, "Do you want to see my room?"

Harlow nodded, and they stood at the same time. Holding her hand, Ryker led them across the room to a hallway lined with doors. About halfway down, he stopped and opened one. Flicking on a light, he tugged her inside and closed the door, pressing Harlow against it. Cupping her cheeks with his big hands, Ryker captured her lips in a searing kiss.

They moved away from the door, and Harlow peeled Ryker's vest off. Right before it hit the floor, he caught it and hung it on a hook on the back of the door.

"Gotta respect the patch," he explained. Harlow had no idea what he meant, her focus on getting him naked. Next, she tugged at the bottom of his black T-shirt and slowly lifted it up, revealing rock hard abs and several scars. She skimmed his bare skin as she lifted the shirt higher. He had a tattoo of a lion's face covering his right pec, the lion's mane transitioning into flames that connected with the ink on his shoulder—a giant skull. His shirt landed on the floor.

With a flick of her fingers, Harlow paused time. Ryker stood before her, frozen. He was shirtless, every defined muscle on display. The man was usually in constant motion and to observe him this way was a rare treat. She dragged her index finger across his chest and down his sculpted abdomen, following the trail of golden-brown hair that disappeared below the waist of his jeans. His skin was tan and covered with tattoos and scars. His body told a story. He was a fighter, a survivor.

She slipped the top of her dress off her shoulders and down her arms. The soft fabric caressed her skin as the dress slid down her body and pooled at her feet. She wasn't wearing a bra, only black lace panties, and these too were cast aside on the floor. Crossing Ryker's room, she tossed the comforter down to the foot of the bed, and she climbed in, lying down on her back right in the middle. The sheets smelled of him, and she moaned when she breathed in his scent.

She snapped her fingers, time resumed, and she watched with amusement as Ryker blinked in confusion when he noticed her clothes on the floor where he last saw her standing. Her giggle gave away her location, and he spun around, his long hair moving with him. Once he saw her there, bare to him, it was like time had frozen still again—only briefly. It took just a few seconds for Ryker to kick off his boots, remove his jeans, and pounce.

Pinned underneath him, she opened her legs wider to cradle his hips. Ryker was already hard and ready, his erection pressed against her, heavy, warm, and throbbing. She moaned, arching so her breasts pressed even closer to his chest. It would have been so easy to have him slide right into her, notching them together, but she didn't want to move that fast. She wanted to savor this night. His eyes changed from stormy blue to gold, and he stared down her at like the master predator he was and she was his prey. *Fuck, that's hot,* she thought, and wrapped her arms around his back, pulling him closer. He growled and burrowed his head into her hair at the crook of her neck. His lips were urgent on her skin, his tongue rough as he sucked, licked, and kissed in that sensitive area. She shuddered and moaned at the sensation. She wanted to writhe, but his body weight limited her movement. She was at his mercy. He licked and sucked his way down to her breasts, drawing a nipple into his mouth. Teeth grazed the sensitive bud, and she cried out. He chuckled, the vibration adding an extra layer of sensation. Harlow's nails dug into his back, and she threw her head back against the pillow with a gasp.

Ryker continued his journey, nipping and sucking at the taut skin on her stomach. Her hands slid into his thick hair as he went lower, his breath hot against her mound. That was the only warning before he was devouring her, lifting her up to meet his mouth. With her hands buried in his hair, she held him there as he sucked her clit and dipped his tongue in deep. His beard scraped against her inner thighs, the burn on her sensitive skin an unexpected turn-on. Nerves were firing little electrical pulses that started in her toes and surged up to where Ryker was owning her pussy. His rough tongue against her clit caused her to twitch and howl. It was like their roles were reversed; Ryker was the one casting a spell and she was turning into a wild animal.

An orgasm surged forth, and Harlow exploded into Ryker's mouth, her nipples almost painful points as her whole body was consumed by desire. Breathless, panting, and boneless, Harlow's arms fell to her sides, releasing their hold on the magnificent man. Ryker grinned at her from between her legs, his eyes still gold, like shimmering jewels. He crawled back up her body, slowly, like he was stalking her and daring her to move. She wasn't going anywhere. His cock bobbed between them, the tip brushing along her thigh, leaving a glistening trail. He was huge, and she wasn't surprised. Everything about Ryker was big—from his towering height and bodybuilder physique to his personality. His presence filled any room, and she couldn't wait for him to fill her.

"I need you," she pleaded, moving a hand to wrap around his length. Now it was his turn to groan. His eyelids fluttered closed as she stroked him. His arms trembled, and she marveled at the fact that she could make this mountain of a man weak from her touch.

"You have me," Ryker growled, then captured her lips with his. The kiss was fierce and hungry. Harlow tasted her juices on his tongue, smelled her essence clinging to his facial hair, and this stoked the flames burning in her blood. Ryker moved so fast, suddenly he was on his back and sliding a condom on before he reached for her, effortlessly lifting her and settling her so she was straddling him. Harlow lowered herself down, taking him inside her slowly as he stretched her wide. It had been a while for her, and once fully seated on him she didn't move, giving her body a chance to adjust. They both moaned with pleasure, and their gazes locked on each other. Ryker's hands trailed down her body, pausing at the curve of her waist before settling on her hips. Holding her in place, he thrust up and slid in even deeper. Harlow gasped and placed a hand on his chest to steady herself before beginning to move, rocking her hips to meet Ryker's subtle thrusts. Electricity hummed and built between them like an approaching storm.

"Oh, my goddess!" she cried out, as it felt like he was growing even bigger and harder as she rode him. Ryker cupped her breasts and tweaked her nipples, increasing the delicious pressure building deep inside. She threw her head back, her long hair tickling the skin on her back. Everything was so sensitive. Ryker's thrusts increased in intensity, and his hands slid back down her sides to hold onto her hips. His grip was tight as he anchored her in place and drove in deeper. Spots danced in her vision as another orgasm washed over her. Reaching behind her, Harlow cupped his balls and squeezed.

"Oh fuck, baby!" Ryker growled, and with a final thrust, he started pulsing inside her as he came. She collapsed on top of him, felt his heart beating against her cheek. Wrapping his arms around her, he held her close, and they stayed joined together until their breathing returned to normal. As weak as a kitten, she managed to climb off of Ryker and lay down next to him. He removed the condom and tossed it in the Denver Broncos trash can next to his bed. With a contented growl, he pulled her into his arms and curled up behind her. From this view she examined his bedroom. In addition to the leather chair, he had an unfinished dresser on the wall between the door and his closet. Another door was propped open, and she saw the edge of a sink vanity and tile floor. He had a few framed posters on the wall. All of motorcycles.

"It's not much," Ryker said, playing with her hair and placing kisses along her shoulder. "But it's the most I've had that I can call my own."

They stayed there in a sated haze. Ryker emitted so much body heat that her bare skin was comfortably warm. His arm was draped over her hip, and his hand was so large that it spanned her abdomen.

"I can't wait until you're swollen with our child," Ryker whispered, pressing his hand against her flat stomach.

His announcement cut through the haze.

"What did you say?" Harlow sat up and pushed free of his embrace. His eyes, now back to their gray blue, narrowed at her reaction.

"You're mine, Harlow Augustine. You're it. I don't want anyone else. I want you. I want to make babies with you and build a home. It may be an unconventional life, but it will be a great life."

He was dead serious, and she felt more exposed than just being naked in his bed. Yes, his unconventional life was what drew her to him. The constraints of being an Augustine were a burden. Expectations were everything, and she was supposed to follow a path plotted out for her. A path she didn't want to follow. Ryker was offering her an alternative, but his declaration was so sudden and unexpected, and way too much, too soon.

"I can't do this," she choked out and scrambled off the bed, narrowly escaping his hand as he reached for her. Flicking her fingers, she froze time again and gathered up her clothes. Once dressed, she crossed to the door and opened it. Before leaving the room, she turned back to look at Ryker. His face bore an expression of hurt and desperation. She almost stopped, unable to bear the guilt knowing she was responsible for that look. He was beautiful and so soft underneath that hard exterior. She swallowed hard as she took in his scars again. A tear spilled down her cheek at the realization that her leaving like this was probably going to break him even more.

Fighting the urge to go back and crawl into the warmth of his arms, to tether herself to him forever, Harlow took a deep, steadying breath and walked out the door. The chaos of the clubhouse was on pause and eerily silent. Monte was leaning over the pool table, his cue poised to shoot a ball into a pocket, while several other patched members stood around watching, unblinking. A club bunny was straddling a man's lap where he was sitting on a sofa near the jukebox. Her tank top was pulled down, and his face was buried in her breasts, his hands gripping her ass. Kai was behind the bar pouring a shot, the liquid frozen in an amber arc that extended from the bottle to the shot glass.

Stepping outside, Harlow carried the spell with her, the coverage and duration of which was beginning to wear on her, so she hurried past the men standing outside by the row of parked motorcycles. They could have been mannequins on display at a Harley dealership. One patched member was frozen in the middle of lighting a cigarette. The flame from his lighter didn't even flicker, and his face was illuminated in its glow.

As soon as Harlow was in her car, she released her spell and sound rushed forth. As she was driving away, she heard Ryker roar. It echoed through the commercial neighborhood, sending birds scattering from the treetops.

~

A week later, Harlow was at work at Coffee Haven and on her third latte with an extra dose of energy tincture, but her ass was still dragging. She hadn't slept much the past few days. Guilt over how she left things with Ryker had her feeling anxious and unsettled.

"I'm such an asshole," she said with a sigh, setting her coffee down to retrieve a tray of scones out of the oven. The morning rush was over, and it was just her and Davis in the shop.

"Okay there?" Davis responded with a lift of an eyebrow. Sensing her mood, he had been giving her a wide berth. Smart man.

The thunder of pipes was unmistakable, and as the roar grew loader, Harlow suspected their destination and braced herself for Ryker's appearance. She'd left his numerous texts and phone calls unanswered, so she fully expected him to walk in the door. She was surprised when Monte walked in, followed by Hunter. They were both wearing jeans and black long-sleeved shirts under their leather vests. While there still wasn't snow on the ground, it was cold enough for it, but these bikers seemed impervious to the weather. Davis moved to stand beside Harlow, tension radiating off of him, and she noticed his hand hovered near a bread knife as if anticipating violence.

"Monte, Hunter," Harlow greeted the SIN brothers. "Can I interest you in a scone? They're fresh out of the oven."

"We need to talk," Hunter growled. "Somewhere private." He eyeballed Davis, who had angled himself so he was partially blocking her.

"Fine." Harlow turned to Davis. "Can I take my break now?"

"Are you going to be okay?" he asked, casting a nervous glance at the two men.

"Yeah, I'm good." Harlow walked out from behind the long marble counter. Hunter followed her through the shop, his heavy boots thudding against the hardwood floors. Monte hung back, and she heard him ordering a scone from Davis. They walked past Willow's office and exited through the rear door that led to the back alley. Harlow turned to face Hunter, crossing her arms over her chest.

"If this is about Ryker, it's none of your business," she spat, because she was disappointed and annoyed that the man wasn't here to confront her himself. Ryker didn't strike her as a cowardly lion.

"Crusher and I prospected together. We got patched together. He's my brother and this is absolutely my business, princess."

"Princess? My name's Harlow. Don't belittle me with some cutesy nickname. And whatever is going on between me and Ryker is between me and Ryker."

Hunter slammed his fist into the brick wall, causing Harlow to flinch, but she didn't back down. "I warned him, you know? You're an Augustine, basically fucking royalty in this town, and I told him he was stupid for even thinking about anything beyond a quick fuck with you. I told him that once you got over your little rebellion and had your taste of slumming it, you'd be gone. Thanks for proving me right."

"It's not like that . . . it's . . . complicated," Harlow stammered, taken aback at how fierce he was being.

"Crusher told me what happened, what he said to you right before you bolted. Bitchy witch move, by the way. Do you know how much it means for a shifter?"

"How much what means?"

"That wasn't just pillow talk or a guy telling a chick what he thinks she wants to hear. A shifter doesn't go around declaring he wants to make babies with just anyone. He wants to mate with you. He's chosen you, princess. Why? I don't fucking know, but if you're who my brother wants, I'll do whatever is in my power to make it happen."

"What are you going to do—force me to be with him? I'm not going to be forced into anything." Harlow was immediately reminded of her grandmother.

"Fuck no. Jesus, between Crusher and myself I've had my hands full with relationship issues. Just talk to him before he rips someone's head off."

"I'll think about it. Is he really that upset?"

Hunter snorted and shook his head. "You have no idea. Just talk to him."

They went back inside, and Harlow noticed Davis scanning her as if checking for bodily harm. She smiled at him as a way to let him know she was fine. It was adorable really. Davis was human and had no idea how well she could defend herself. Monte was sitting at a table, his long legs stretched out before him. There were some black scuff marks on the floor from his boots. He had a pumpkin spiced latte in a cardboard to-go cup and was stuffing a blueberry scone in his face.

"Bro," he said to Hunter. "You gotta get one of these, man. They're fucking delicious."

As soon as they left, Harlow fished her phone out of her bag that she kept in Willow's office and texted Ryker.

Harlow: I'm sorry. Can we talk? My place tonight at 7? I'll make dinner.

Ryker: Yeah. I'll be there.

She put her phone down and exhaled. At least he responded, and Hunter was right. Ryker deserved an explanation.

That night she was in her kitchen, putting the finishing touches on a batch of yakisoba, when she heard the familiar sound of a motorcycle. Her heart started to race, and she took a few calming breaths. She ran her hands through her hair and smoothed her sweater as she walked to the front door, opening it before Ryker could knock. Harlow let out a gasp when she saw him.

He looked like hell. His hair was unkempt, and his eyes were bloodshot. His stubble had grown out and was approaching a full beard. The facial hair didn't hide his split bottom lip. He eyed her warily when he stepped past her and into her house. He was cold, distant, and she didn't blame him. She had done that. Where he had been so open, he was now closed off. She hated it.

He remembered to take off his boots, and afterward, he followed her into the kitchen. She offered him bourbon, having bought a bottle of his favorite brand. He nodded and looked around as she poured him a glass. Her bedroom was right off the kitchen, and the door was open. He peered inside, and she noticed his nostrils flaring as he sniffed the air.

"So there isn't someone else?" he asked, taking the drink from her hand.

"What? No. I'm not seeing anyone else."

He nodded. "I didn't smell anyone here except you . . . and your familiar."

Ryker glanced down, and Harlow followed suit. Mamoru was sniffing Ryker's feet again.

She served up bowls of yakisoba, piling an extra helping onto Ryker's, and brought them over to the bistro table that was near the window with a view of her backyard.

Ryker moved the chopsticks to the side and picked up a fork, shoveling a forkful of noodles into his mouth. He growled in approval and took another bite. "So why?"

"Why what?" Harlow asked.

"Why did you fucking run?"

With a sigh, Harlow set her chopsticks down and dabbed at the corner of her mouth with a napkin. "I like you, Ryker. But when you started talking about babies and settling down . . . I freaked out. I'm not ready for that. We're still getting to know each other. I have a lot going on right now and don't even know if I want a serious relationship. My last one ended badly."

"Your ex cheated on you?" Harlow nodded and looked down at her bowl. "Monte reminded me that you're not a shifter and wouldn't get the mating instinct. I didn't want to listen. It wouldn't be the first time someone I care about has left me."

"Ouch." Harlow winced at the reference to Ryker's mother abandoning him. "I deserve that, and I'm sorry."

Ryker shrugged and picked up his glass, draining the rest of the bourbon in two gulps. He set the glass down on the table, and when he looked at her, his irises were ringed with gold. "I don't date. I can't tell you the last time I had a girlfriend. I avoid getting close because . . . well, you know my history. Getting close means getting burned."

"Trust me, I know, and I've been there."

He scratched at his beard and regarded her from across the table. "I'm willing to give you time and space. For you." Harlow started to smile, and she sat up straighter until he said, "Just know that you're it for me. I know it and my animal knows it."

"Now see, you say shit like that, and it makes me freak out. You gotta dial it back, dude."

He scowled, but then she saw his lips quirk up. "Dude?" He laughed and shook his head. "I'll try to tone it down, but only expect honesty from me. I tell it like it is."

"Honesty is good." She reached across the table and tucked her hand in his, giving it a squeeze. "I'll be honest with you, too."

After they finished eating, Ryker had to leave. He was needed at the clubhouse. That's when he told her that club business was one thing he couldn't talk to her about, unless he had permission.

"Why?" she asked, her eyes narrowing with suspicion.

"That's just how it is, out of respect to the brotherhood." Ryker stood up from where he had been tying his boots. When he saw her standing with her arms crossed over her chest and giving him the stink eye, he chuckled.

"Come here, Country Club."

Closing the space between them, he cupped her face with his hands and gently ran a thumb along her bottom lip. She uncrossed her arms and stepped closer, her gaze not wavering from his. She ran her hands underneath his vest, enjoying the flex of his muscles and the heat coming off his body. Tilting her head, she licked her lips, drawing Ryker's attention. His eyes, more gold than blue, stared hungrily at her mouth before capturing it with a kiss. His mouth moved over hers slowly, his beard surprisingly soft where it brushed against her skin. Suddenly he broke off the kiss and rested his forehead against hers. She noticed he was panting.

"I want to take you against this wall or bend you over your couch, baby. I want to fill you, mark you as mine right here and right now," he growled. His hands that were still cupping her cheeks trembled, letting her know how much he was holding back. "If we don't stop now, I won't be able to stop. I want you to be sure about us. When you're ready, you let me know."

Ryker placed a kiss on her forehead and stepped away, opening the front door. His boots thudded as he crossed the porch, and Harlow watched his retreat, her lips still tingling from their kiss.

This is for the best, right?

CHAPTER 6

TWO MONTHS LATER

*T*he bell above the door chimed, and Harlow looked over to see a petite woman walking through, her face hidden by a giant bouquet of red and white roses. The bouquet was set down on the counter, and Willow's mom appeared from behind, wearing a huge smile. Her cheeks were extra rosy from the cold, a bloom of color against her porcelain skin.

Harlow rolled her eyes. "Let me guess, Ryker sent these?"

Reagan Fairchild, Willow's mom, co-owned Fairy Tale Florists, and she usually had an employee handle deliveries, but she took any opportunity to drop in at Coffee Haven to see her daughter and grab a cup of coffee. Ryker had been giving her plenty of opportunities over the past two months. Once a week he ordered flowers to be delivered to Harlow. Willow's mom couldn't get enough of the big biker's romantic side.

"He sure did." Reagan handed her a small envelope. "Oh, Harlow, you should see him. He has no idea what to do, and the flowers sometimes make him sneeze. It's adorable. He's smart, though, and figured out to leave the bouquet choice up to us."

Harlow chuckled, picturing Ryker, all six feet five inches of him in his leathers, surrounded by flowers. Picking up a bread knife, she sliced the top of the envelope open and pulled out the card.

These petals are as soft as your skin. Their fragrance is not nearly as sweet as your scent. My heart races thinking of you. I miss you. Happy Valentine's Day.

Yours, Ryker

A flush washed over her body when she read his intimate message written in his cramped handwriting. She'd had no idea that a romantic was hiding beneath the rough exterior. True to his word, Ryker had slowed things down. He had been busy with his three jobs and club business. She had been busy straight through the holidays. Despite their schedules, Ryker found time to woo her while still giving her space. In addition to the weekly flowers, she had come home one day to find a stuffed lion on her porch with a sweet note attached. That lion had been in her bed ever since. She fell asleep hugging it to her chest, and she would dream of Ryker, dreams so vivid she woke up disappointed to find herself alone. Other gifts he left for her showed how much he had been paying attention during their brief time together: white sage candles for her meditation room, a cookbook with fusion recipes, her favorite tea, and her favorite lotion from Madame Tahini's Potions, Lotions, and Palm Readings.

"Harlow, I'm not one to meddle, but this guy has it bad for you. While I enjoy the business, when are you going to put him out of his lovesick misery?" Reagan asked.

"He isn't lovesick."

"Honey, I can feel him pining away, and I'm not even empathic like my daughter. Speaking of, is Willow in her office?"

"No, she ran to the bank."

"Oh, I'll go catch up with her. Don't let that poor boy wait too long," she said before leaving, holding the door open for Shayna, who whistled when she saw the bouquet.

"Damn, girl, he's not giving up, is he? I agree with Willow's mom."

Harlow groaned and set about making her friend a latte. "Not you too. You know I'm not ready."

"Bullshit. You're scared of getting hurt again and of what your family thinks. You need to do you, Harlow. You only live once."

"You did not just YOLO me," Harlow teased when she handed Shayna her coffee.

"I sure as hell did!" Shayna winked at her before taking a sip. She closed her eyes and sighed. "God, I needed this. Listen, I gotta get back to the medical center, but we're not done talking about this."

Shayna left, and Harlow was surprisingly alone in Coffee Haven. Taking advantage of the rare lull, she sat down at one of the tables by the window. Harlow read Ryker's card again, then she thought about what Shayna said. Her friend knew her too well. She stood up and walked to the back of the shop where she kept her bag in Willow's office. Pulling out her phone, she texted Ryker.

Harlow: Thank you for the roses. They're beautiful. I miss you too.

She immediately followed up with a second text:

Harlow: I'm ready.

Harlow slipped the phone into the back pocket of her jeans and went back up to the counter to start closing down. She was washing one of the coffee urns when her phone buzzed. She couldn't dry her hand fast enough and left a streak of moisture on the screen when she unlocked it. Ryker had texted her back.

Ryker: Thank fuck! I've been goin out of my mind. Do you have plans tonight?

At first, she wanted to tease him and tell him she had a Valentine's date, but she didn't. He had been patient long enough. Instead she replied:

Harlow: Hopefully I do now?

It didn't take long to make plans. He would bring takeout and meet her at her house. She didn't want a fancy night out. Most places in town would be booked anyway. She had no desire to go to the Cupids and Cuties party at Whisper Falls Inn, either. All Harlow wanted was to see Ryker. Now that she had made up her mind, she wondered why she had waited so long.

Harlow had just stepped out of the shower when the doorbell rang. Not wanting Ryker to stand outside in the cold, she slipped on her robe and went to answer the door. There he stood on the porch, larger than ever and holding a pizza from Napoli's. They stared at each other, not saying anything at first. Harlow didn't know what to say, suddenly feeling shy. Would jumping his bones right away be appropriate? He certainly was more appealing than the pizza. Dark denim jeans hugged his thighs and hung on his hips. He wore a Harley Davidson hoodie underneath his cut. His beard was shorter and more groomed than the last time she saw him. His hair was pulled back and way too tame.

"Hi," she managed to say and stepped backwards, making room for Ryker to come inside. He set the pizza down on the small table by her coat rack. It balanced precariously on her keys but didn't slide off onto the floor. In one swift movement, she was swept up in his arms, and Ryker was kissing her. He nipped at her bottom lip, and his hands slid down her back to grab her ass, pressing her against him. Her silk robe clung to her damp skin, and his touch was so hot she imagined steam would rise from her body. The material was thin, and she wasn't wearing anything underneath, which meant she felt everything. The pizza was long forgotten. They were both too hungry for each other.

Ryker set Harlow down and took a step back, tugging on the sash that held her robe closed. The knot loosened and her robe parted. His golden eyes flashed as he took in her naked body, and he licked his lips, nostrils flaring as he breathed her scent in, looking every bit the lion. He traced a finger from her neck down, swirling around a nipple until it tightened into a hard point. She swayed into his touch as he continued past her stomach at a leisurely, teasing pace. She let out a sigh when his finger finally slipped between her folds.

"Fuck, babe, you're already so wet," he growled as he stroked her clit, his calloused thumb running over the sensitive bud. "I can't wait. We'll go nice and slow next time."

Ryker backed Harlow up until she was against the sofa and then he spun her around and bent her over, lifting her robe up until it pooled on her back. The air was cool on her ass but not for long. Ryker's jeans hit the floor, she heard the tear of a condom wrapper, and then he was pushing inside her with a grunt. She gasped at the fullness and how warm he was as he slid in deep. Having her bent over this way gave him all the control. He wrapped her ponytail around his hand, simultaneously holding her in place and pulling her closer to where they were joined. He fucked her hard and fast, and she met his every thrust, until she came apart with a cry and her legs threatened to stop supporting her. Sensing this, Ryker wrapped an arm around her waist, and raising her up higher, he continued moving. She felt every ridge as he slid in and out, pushing deeper every time. Tightening around him, increasing the sensation, did them both in, and when Ryker released, his pulses triggered another orgasm. Harlow collapsed face first into her sofa, Ryker draped over her, panting hot air onto the back of her neck. They stayed like that for a few minutes, catching their breath.

Later that night they were lying in bed, clothes discarded on the floor. Harlow was curled up next to Ryker, her head resting on his chest. She traced his lion tattoo with her finger, her eyelids growing heavy.

"I have to go to Denver," Ryker said, breaking the silence and bringing Harlow back from the brink of sleep. "There's a supernatural fight club where I used to be one of the elite fighters before I moved to Havenwood Falls. There's somebody I need to talk to there . . . club business."

"When do you have to go?" Harlow asked, looking up at him. Ryker had been open about his past. This information about him fighting in some supernatural fight club was new but not surprising. The fact that he was an elite fighter didn't surprise her either. If he had claim to a pride, he for sure would be the alpha.

"As soon as possible. Would you be able to go with me? We can make a getaway out of it—hotel, room service, and no one bothering us." Ryker's hands began to roam, small strokes along her spine until he was squeezing her ass, pressing her body closer to his. They were already naked, and just that small touch . . .

CHAPTER 7

Two days later, they were in Denver. The location for the fights that Saturday night was an abandoned warehouse on the edge of the city—away from prying eyes. Sections of the roof were missing, which meant there were patches of snow covering parts of the cracked concrete floor. Ryker had told Harlow that Fuzzbert, the troll who ran the fights, preferred locations that accommodated avian creatures, like dragons. Sometimes a fight would be held in an alley in the city. With enough glamours in place, passersby wouldn't notice anything amiss.

They arrived early in hopes of talking to Fuzzbert ahead of the fights. Following Ryker's suggestion, Harlow hung back and let Ryker do the talking. He and the troll had a history. She was fascinated by the crowd that was beginning to gather—a cross section of supernaturals placing bets on the first match, which was a vampire versus an Unseelie fae.

"My grandmother and the Court would stroke out if something like this was held in Havenwood Falls," she said.

"We have fight nights at the clubhouse. I'm pretty sure the Court's aware. The Bishops and even Addie have fought before."

"Are you serious?" Harlow looked up at him in disbelief, and Ryker shrugged.

"What? They don't have that at the country club?" he teased, and she smacked his arm.

Fuzzbert was hard to miss. A seven-foot troll with a wart-covered nose the size of an eggplant stood out, even in the crowd that contained ogres and a griffin. Ryker finally got Fuzzbert's undivided attention, so Harlow stopped people-watching to listen.

"Stray! What are you doing here? It's been a while. Are you here to fight? I'm sure I can get you a match." Fuzzbert's voice was huskier than a smoker's with a sore throat.

"Nah, those days are over. I'm actually here on club business." He gestured at his cut. "I'm checking in with other supernatural communities in Colorado to see if anyone's seen this woman." Ryker held out a picture. "Have you seen her before?"

Fuzzbert's bulbous eyes narrowed. "Nah. Can she fight?"

"Yeah. She's a known associate of the Collector. Does that name ring a bell?"

"Not that I know of."

Ryker handed him the picture. He had written his phone number on the back. "Call me if you see this woman, okay? And keep your distance from her—she's dangerous."

Fuzzbert stared at the paper in Ryker's hand and didn't take it. "Whatever it is, I don't want to be involved. Every troll for himself, you know what I mean?"

"I get it. If you change your mind, I'll make it worth your while. Me and my girl are going to hang and watch for a bit. She's never been and is curious." Ryker started to walk away when Fuzzbert called after him.

"There is someone here you'll want to talk to—he'll be fighting the winner of this match."

"Is this about the woman?"

"No. You. He's been looking for you. Claims he's your brother. I don't know. He looks like you and fights like you, too. Not as fierce, but he's young and learning. Reminds me so much of you that I've taken to calling him Stray Jr."

Harlow noticed the tension in Ryker's stance and saw he was clenching his fists. "I don't have a brother."

"Hey, that's what this guy's been saying. Might be worth your while to stick around and find out."

Ryker joined Harlow and clasped her hand, holding it tighter than usual.

"Are you okay?" she asked.

"I guess it's possible that I have a brother. I don't know what happened to my mom after she abandoned me."

On their first date, Ryker told her how he never researched his mom after he was out of foster care. She had abandoned him, and he didn't want to chase her if she didn't want him.

"And if this man is your brother?"

Ryker licked his lips and looked down at her, hope lighting up his eyes. "Then he's my brother, and we have a lot of catching up to do."

The vampire won the first match. He managed to pin the fae down and latched onto a vein, slowly draining him dry in front of a stunned audience. The Unseelie had been favored to win. After the match, the vampire was juiced and moving faster than ever. Fae blood was like an amphetamine to vamps. He raced around the center of the warehouse in a blur as Fuzzbert called Stray Jr. in to fight.

"Why Stray?" Harlow asked Ryker, who snorted in response.

"Fuzzbert has a sense of humor. I'm a lion, so a cat, and I was homeless—no family."

"Oh, a stray cat. I get it. That's really not that funny."

"No." Ryker's focus was pulled to the center of the warehouse, where a lion stood poised to fight. Harlow had only seen Ryker in his lion form once. He had shifted for her in the clubhouse right before they left for Denver, and he was glorious. The lion getting ready to fight was leaner, and his mane wasn't as resplendent. The vampire drew first blood. He moved so fast that it was impossible to see when he struck. One minute the lion was crouched, ready to pounce, and the next minute, he had a gaping bite wound on his left shoulder.

"The vamp is juiced and has an unfair advantage. Fuzzbert should never have allowed this fight," Ryker growled, his eyes flashing gold and nostrils flaring as he struggled to contain his cat.

He paced in front of Harlow, anxiously watching the fight. The lion was watching his opponent though, and as if counting down in his head how long it took from the moment the vampire disappeared to the time it struck last time, the lion was ready. Swiping with a paw the size of a baseball mitt, he hit the vampire, slashing deep cuts in its chest. Blood sprayed out across the concrete floor, and the crowd cheered. While the vampire's wounds closed almost immediately, the lion's wound was still bleeding. A sluggish flow, but fresh blood nonetheless, which served as a beacon for vampires. As Harlow looked around the crowd, she saw several vamps with their fangs dropped, eyeing the lion hungrily.

The two fighters circled each other, each waiting to make the next move. Harlow started chewing on the corner of her fingernail from the anticipation. When the vampire disappeared again, her heart jumped in her throat. He reappeared on the back of the lion, his fangs embedded deep in the lion's neck. The lion bucked and roared, trying to shake the parasite loose, but the vampire held on like he was a professional bull rider.

"Roll!" Ryker bellowed. "Roll, god damn it!"

The lion must have heard him, because he did just that. He rolled, and his weight caused the vampire to loosen his hold enough that when the lion was back on all four paws, he could shake him off. Stray Jr. was weak, though, and stumbled slightly. The vampire had managed to drain a lot of blood.

Harlow couldn't bear to watch anymore. Ryker was right—the vampire had an unfair advantage. She couldn't imagine what Ryker was experiencing. This could be his brother, and he was watching him growing weaker by the minute.

Then it was over. The vampire practically flew through the air, landing with such impact on the lion that his front legs collapsed under him. The vampire struck like a cobra and buried his fangs in deep. The lion struggled to regain his footing but was too weak. Within seconds, his eyes closed, and the magnificent animal slumped as the last of his life was drained from him. The crowd roared and cheered. Harlow and Ryker were completely silent as they watched the lion transform back to human. A naked man covered in blood lay on the concrete. Even from where they were standing, Harlow could see the resemblance, and horror washed over her. Then Ryker was running, yelling at the trolls who had come to clear the body away.

Harlow was right behind him and helped to push people aside as Ryker sunk to his knees beside the dead man. She glanced down at his face and gasped. It was like looking at a younger version of Ryker. The jaw wasn't as square, and his hair darker, but there was no denying the resemblance.

"Oh, my goddess." She joined Ryker and reached for him, but he angrily pulled away.

Fuzzbert had arrived to see what all the commotion was, and

Ryker rounded on him. "You should have called the fight, Fuzz! You know that was a dirty play."

The troll laughed his smoker's laugh. "Stray, you know the rules of Supernatural Fight Club. No weapons, only abilities. The vamp used his abilities to his advantage."

"What was his real name?" Ryker growled. "At least give me that."

"I don't know it. Maybe someone else does?" Fuzzbert asked the small crowd that had gathered around them.

An older man stepped forward. He was holding a plastic shopping bag. "This is the boy's. He checked this in before the fight."

He handed the bag to Ryker, and Harlow peered inside when he opened it. There was a pair of jeans that were frayed at the ankles, a blue hoodie, a pair of black Converse, and on top, a wallet. Grabbing the wallet, Ryker opened it and pulled out a driver's license.

"Holy fuck."

He fell to his knees. Harlow looked over his shoulder and saw an Arizona license, but the name made her throat thick with emotion: Orion Pride. The look of devastation on Ryker's face was too much to bear. How cruel was fate to deliver a blood brother to him, only to snatch him away before they had a chance to know each other? She would do anything to take that pain from him. If only she could turn back time.

That's when it hit her. She could turn back time. Her grandmother had warned her against it, but why would Harlow be given the power if she wasn't meant to use it? She could help Ryker. Give him the family he'd always wanted. She loved him and would give him the world. *Oh, my goddess, I love him!*

Thinking back to the spell she saw written in the family

grimoire, Harlow recited the verse in her head repeatedly before speaking the words out loud. First, she waved her hand then whispered the spell to stop time. Everything came to a complete halt. In the silence, she concentrated on the spell. She had to concentrate to go far back enough to prevent death from happening again.

With her arms raised in the air, she closed her eyes and tilted her head back, calling her words out for the universe to hear. Wind began to howl, and her hair lifted up. It was like she was caught in the middle of a tornado, and she was seeing images of the recent events whipping by. When she saw the part where Ryker and Fuzzbert were talking, she stopped.

"I mote it done. Blessed be," she said and sound erupted around her as everything around her resumed. Sweat dripped down the back of her neck, and a wave a dizziness almost caused her to fall over. Struggling to get her wits about her, Harlow focused on the conversation Ryker was having with Fuzzbert.

"There is someone here you'll want to talk to—he'll be fighting the winner of this match."

"Is this about the woman?"

"No. You. He's been looking for you. Claims he's your brother. I don't know. He looks like you and fights like you, too. Not as fierce, but he's young and learning. Reminds me so much of you that I've taken to calling him Stray Jr."

Now Harlow had to act fast to keep the match with Ryker's little brother from happening. She frantically looked around for some ideas. The area they were in was deserted. Nothing surrounded the abandoned warehouse except for several cars in the parking lot, Ryker's Bronco included. *Think, Harlow, think!* She muttered to herself, panic beginning to set in as she was running out of time. The vampire and fae fight had already begun. Then inspiration struck. Calling upon her elemental magic, she borrowed fire when someone used a lighter to light their cigarette. By the time the flame hit one of the cars in the parking lot, it was a fireball. She sent another, and a second car caught fire. Chaos ensued as supes scattered to check on their vehicles. The fight stopped, and Fuzzbert's shouts were falling on deaf ears.

Ryker started to run toward his Bronco, but Harlow stopped him. "I'll go. You find Stray Jr. Now's your chance to find out if he's really your brother."

She was practically swaying on her feet, the amount of magic Harlow had used taking its toll. She felt like she could curl up on the ground and sleep for days. She staggered across the uneven parking lot, each step requiring all the energy she had left. Harlow made it to the Bronco and sat down heavily on the back bumper. She looked up and saw Ryker walking toward her, grinning and with his brother by his side. She knew it was worth it.

"Harlow, meet Orion. My brother." Ryker beamed with joy, and Harlow felt the sting of tears in her eyes at seeing that joy.

"Nice to meet you," she said. Seeing them standing side by side, there was no doubt they were brothers. Orion was a little shorter, and his eyes were hazel ringed with gold. Those were the only major differences. "Let's get out of here. You guys have some serious catching up to do."

"Do you have a car here?" Ryker asked Orion.

"Nah, I ran here. Haven't been able to afford a car just yet."

"Good. Ride with us, and we can talk."

Harlow climbed into the back, giving the brothers the front seat. She practically collapsed and stretched out on the bench. She closed her eyes and half drifted in and out of sleep as she listened to them talking.

She learned that the brothers shared the same mother but had different fathers. Both were unknown, and the half-brothers had their mother's surname. Jeanine Pride died in April 2015 when Orion was sixteen. From there, he was placed in foster care. When he was released on his eighteenth birthday, he was handed an envelope from his mom that revealed he had an older half-brother named Ryker whom she had abandoned. Inside the envelope was a child's shirt sealed in a plastic bag to preserve Ryker's scent. With just a name and a scent, Orion was able to track his brother to Denver.

"How long have you been looking for me?" Ryker asked.

"A little over a year. I turned nineteen in November."

"Jesus, man. I'm glad we found each other."

"Me too."

Harlow fell asleep after that. The murmur of male voices lulled her to sleep. She woke up when they arrived back at the hotel.

"Orion's going to stay with us. We have the sofa that pulls out to a bed in the room."

"Of course." Her eyes drifted closed again. She didn't have the energy to keep them open.

"Babe, are you okay?" Ryker's voice was close to her ear, and she realized he was carrying her.

"So tired," she managed to say, and that's the last thing she remembered. When she woke the next morning, she was still wearing her jeans and sweater from the day before. Ryker was sprawled out beside her in his boxer briefs. Light snoring from across the room caught her attention, and she looked over to see Orion sprawled out on the sofa bed, his feet hanging off the end. He was in boxers and a ratty Metallica T-shirt that she recognized as Ryker's.

"Hey, are you feeling better?"

Harlow turned her head to find Ryker's blue gaze fixed on her.

He was lying on his side facing her, one hand tucked underneath his pillow.

"I'm good. Just needed sleep." She hated not telling him the truth. They had made a promise to be honest with each other and not keep secrets. But no one could know what she did. Bringing Orion back crossed so many lines—ethical and natural.

CHAPTER 8

Orion returned to Havenwood Falls with them. Ryker had called ahead to let Liam Peters, the president of SIN, know, and he was going to make arrangements for Orion to be vetted by the Court. After a string of recent attacks on the town, the Court had issued a lockdown of sorts. All new supes entering the wards needed to be cleared by Elsmed Fairchild. His ability to read minds expedited the process. Harlow made sure to stay far away during that interview. She didn't need Elsmed poking around in her brain and discovering what happened.

Fortunately, Orion passed with flying colors. Harlow offered her guest room to him, and he moved in. He traveled light and came to town with only one duffel bag. Clothes, his birth certificate, and a few pictures were all he owned. Everything was going great. Orion was settling in, and he and Ryker quickly formed a bond. Then Taylor came over.

Harlow thought that with Taylor and Orion being the same age, Taylor could show Orion around and introduce him to other supes their age.

"Are you sure you didn't bring me to heaven, Harlow? Because your sister is an angel." Orion flirted shamelessly with her sister, and Taylor took it in stride by rolling her eyes.

"I can introduce you to an angel, if you want. But he's a dude."

Chuckling at her sister's spicy response, Harlow left them in the living room and went to the kitchen for a glass of water.

"There's something wrong," Taylor said from right behind her. Harlow jumped and almost dropped her glass.

"What's wrong?"

"Not what—who. Orion, there's something wrong with him," Taylor whispered, looking over her shoulder to make sure he hadn't followed her in. "Can we go upstairs and talk? You know you can do the soundproofing spell."

After setting her glass on the counter, Harlow followed Taylor upstairs to her meditation room. Harlow recited a soundproofing spell so their conversation couldn't be heard outside of the room.

"Taylor, what is going on?"

"You know how I can see spirits and talk to the dead? Well, I can see death on Orion. He's been dead before. Darkness clings to him."

"Shit." Harlow sunk down to the floor and cradled her head in her hands. Laughter echoed up the stairs from below. Even their laugh was the same, and since Orion had showed up, Ryker was laughing a lot more. His happiness made her heart full.

"Harlow, what do you know?"

Charles was dead then I changed time, and he was whole again, as if his death didn't happen, except he was altered. Death should remain final. Harlow remembered the warning from her great-great-aunt Lucille's notes—a warning she chose to ignore.

"If I tell you, you have to sister swear that you won't repeat any of this to anyone. Do you swear?"

"I swear." Taylor sat down cross-legged on the floor, and Harlow told her sister everything.

"Holy shit," Taylor said when Harlow finished. "So you don't know what happened to Charles for Lucille to issue such a warning?"

"I don't. All Grandma said was that their romance ended in tragedy."

"So we have no idea what Orion might become." Taylor chewed on her lip and tapped her finger against her leg, things she did whenever she was deep in thought. "Tell you what. I'll keep an eye on the darkness that's attached to Orion. If it gets worse, we'll figure out what to do. In the meantime, he's staying here, so you can watch him. Look for any strange behaviors."

"Thanks, Tay." Harlow hugged her sister, holding on to her longer than usual.

Life resumed, and by mid-March, nothing unusual had happened. Orion was even considering prospecting for the MC. Harlow began to sleep a little easier. Surely if something was going to happen, it would have happened already.

The night of the full moon and first day of spring, Harlow and Ryker had the house to themselves. Orion had gone out hunting with Kai Reynolds. The two teens had hit it off, and Ryker trusted Kai to not let anything happen to his brother.

The spring equinox coinciding with a supermoon affected all of the supernaturals differently. Where Orion was drawn to hunt, Ryker wanted to fuck, and so did Harlow. She felt twitchy and antsy. The moment they were alone, Ryker scooped Harlow up and carried her into her bedroom. The few seconds it took for him to set her on the bed gave her enough time to cast a spell that caused their clothes to disappear from their bodies and reappear on the floor.

"That's a handy trick," Ryker said, before covering her with his body and kissing her deeply. Harlow wrapped her legs around his hips, crossing her ankles right above his ass to hold him in place as he slid inside and filled her. Ryker hovered over her, muscles rippling as he rocked his hips forward in deep, steady thrusts. He stared down at her, and she stared back, unable to look away from the intensity of his glowing gold eyes. Shifting to support his weight on one arm, he cupped her breast. The heat of his palm seeped into her skin, a slow sensual burn that accelerated when he rolled her nipple between calloused fingers. This sent a straight shock to where their bodies were joined.

"Oh my goddess, yes!" Harlow closed her eyes and cried out, pressing her head back into the pile of pillows. Her hips rose to meet his—in an attempt to ease or increase the pressure, she didn't know. All she knew was that she was so close to the edge, but Ryker controlled the pace, and he was taking his time. Harlow opened up her eyes and was getting ready to beg for release when she noticed the intensity of his gaze had shifted. He looked upon her almost reverently.

"Do you know how much I love you?" he asked.

"As much as I love you," she responded. This was the first time she let him know her true feelings for him. Her family was going to have to get used to Ryker being around, because she wasn't giving him up for anything. She had already moved time for him.

"Oh, baby, say it again," he begged and thrust into her, making her moan.

"I love you!"

He smiled down at her before devouring her lips. They moved together, making love to each other, and ended up a tangle of limbs. Their bliss was interrupted by Ryker's cell phone. He groaned and rolled over to grab his phone out of his jeans pocket.

"Prospect, what's going on?" Ryker sat up, and Harlow

couldn't help but admire the way his abs tightened with each movement. "What do you mean—wait, slow down." The change of tone caused Harlow to look at Ryker, who was on the move again. He stood up and started pulling his jeans on. "I'll be right there. No. Don't tell anyone else."

"Babe, what happened?" Harlow got up too and started getting dressed.

"Apparently Orion snapped and attacked someone."

"What?" She rushed out of the bedroom, following Ryker as he tugged on his boots and grabbed his keys from the table by the front door.

"I don't know. Kai said he was fine one minute and the next he was completely out of control."

Harlow froze mid-step, realizing this was her fault. This was that moment she had been dreading. Her magic had consequences, and someone was hurt because of it. More people were going to be hurt when they found out what she did.

"Let's go to him," she said. She'd tell him later. She'd confess even if it meant losing him. Even if it meant losing everything.

CHAPTER 9

*N*ot knowing what they were walking into, Ryker grabbed a change of clothes and a pair of boots from Orion's room while Harlow gathered up extra blankets and a few bottles of water. They dressed for the cold night, packed up the Bronco, and drove out of town. Kai and Orion had gone past the wards to go hunting, and Kai was waiting for them at a gas station located on the outskirts of Eldredge, a small town less than an hour north of Havenwood Falls and near the Ridgway Reservoir. The reservoir was a popular water source for wildlife. Perfect hunting grounds for a lion and a vampire. Hunting beyond the wards added a bit of a rush, too. The risk of getting caught heightened the experience.

They pulled into the gas station, parking in a dark corner, just out of reach of the lights from the pumps. Kai seemed to melt out of the shadows. Wearing all black and with his dark hair, his pale face appeared first. He climbed into the back seat and gave Ryker directions.

"I'm sorry, Crusher. He was beyond reason and so strong. Tossed me against a tree, and I thought he broke my fucking back." Harlow twisted around to look at Kai, and he definitely wasn't his usual put-together self. There were a few leaves in his dark hair, and his jacket sleeve was almost torn off. "I ran until I got cell service and called you."

"You did good, prospect." Ryker concentrated on the road, turning onto a narrow dirt road that had more ruts than smooth sections. Harlow was glad they were in the Bronco. Had they taken her Mini, they would have broken an axle a mile back.

"Stop here," Kai barked from the back, and Ryker slammed on the brakes. They stopped behind a pickup truck that had a missing tailgate and bumper sticker declaring the owner loved the Second Amendment. "This truck belongs to the guy Orion killed. I recognize his scent."

"How far of a hike is it in to get to the scene?" Ryker asked, getting out of the truck and beginning to strip off his clothes, placing them on the driver's seat. He was sniffing the air, his nostrils flaring.

"Not far. About a mile through the trees that way." Kai pointed to the west.

"What the fuck is someone doing out here alone? It's not like this is ideal camping weather, and it's not hunting season."

"The guy looked like a hunter. Maybe he was a poacher?" Kai suggested. This caused Ryker to growl.

"Babe, do you want hang back here? Kai and I can handle this." Ryker's eyes flickered gold. His lion was close to the surface.

"Not a chance." Harlow tightened her ponytail, secured the hood of her parka, and pulled on a pair of ski gloves. She grabbed the bag that contained the blankets, water, and clothes, slinging it over her shoulder.

"I'm not talking you out of this, am I?"

"Nope."

Ryker shook his head and muttered something about

stubborn-ass witches before shifting. Harlow winced, as it sounded like his muscles were tearing as his body morphed into his majestic beast. Seconds later, a lion stood in the clearing. It had started to flurry, and snowflakes collected on his golden-brown mane and immediately evaporated. He chuffed, raised his head into the air, and sniffed before running into the woods. His big paws barely made a sound.

Kai lifted the bag off of Harlow's shoulders and secured it on his.

"Ready to run?" he asked. "Crusher is on a mission."

"Let's go."

Kai could have run a lot faster, but he kept even with Harlow, and she suspected he provided protection as part of his prospect duties. She wasn't a slouch and had been running her entire life. A mile run through the woods was nothing. Ryker's tracks were easy to follow in the snow, and it didn't take long for them to reach the campsite.

"Oh, my goddess." Harlow bent over and gasped like someone had punched her in the stomach. The pizza from Napoli's she had eaten for dinner threatened to come back up as she took in the scene before her.

The man was dead. There was no surviving the devastation that had happened to his body. Parts were missing. His left arm had been completely ripped off and lay in a puddle of bloody slush several feet away. Entrails spilled out from where his stomach had been slashed open. The man's right leg smoldered in what remained of the campfire he had been huddled around. Harlow's stomach turned again when she realized it wasn't barbecue she had smelled. Sure enough, a hunting rifle was propped against his cooler. He hadn't had a chance to reach for it.

Bloody paw prints, slightly smaller than Ryker's, were everywhere. But Orion was nowhere to be found.

"Go find him," Harlow told Ryker. "I've got this. It's my mess, and I should be the one to clean it up."

Ryker tilted his head and narrowed his gold ringed eyes. Harlow knew he would have questions once he was back in his human form, and she'd answer them honestly.

"What does that mean?" Kai asked.

Harlow shook her head. "Long story. Stand back. I'm going to work my magic."

Just as Harlow raised her hands in the air to clean up evidence that would link the animal attack to an African lion, which would surely raise questions with the game warden, Kai shouted at her to look out. She spun around to see a lion charging at her, Ryker right on his tail. Orion's maw was soaked in blood, and his eyes were bottomless dark pools. He pounced, and Harlow fell backward, bracing herself for his crushing weight, but then her magic responded. Orion froze midair, his razor-sharp, two-inch-long canines inches from her face. Her magic had risen in self-defense, like from muscle memory.

Ryker slid to a stop beside her, the muscles along his side rippling under his fur as he breathed heavily. He nuzzled against her chest, bumping her with his nose, checking her for injuries. She buried her hands in his mane and told him she was okay. She stood up to show him she was unscathed. He chuffed and bumped her again, forcing her to move.

"You want me out of the way?" she asked, and he dipped his head, which she assumed meant yes. She stood off the side, and Kai positioned himself in front of her as Ryker stood in front of his brother, ready to face off.

"Should I release him?" she called across the clearing, and Ryker chuffed. She did, and the two lions clashed. Their roars echoed into the night, raising the hair on her arms. Ryker managed to get his teeth into Orion's neck and brought him to the ground, where he thrashed, clawing at Ryker with all four paws, but Ryker held on, forcing his brother to submit.

Minutes later, Orion was back in his human form, and his naked body was curled up in a fetal position. He was covered in blood and trembling. Kai rushed forward and draped a blanket over him. Ryker shifted back and crouched next to Orion.

"Bro, what happened?" Ryker asked his little brother.

"I—I don't know. The urge to kill just came over me. I've never hurt a human before and that . . ." Orion stared at the macabre scene of his creation and started to sob. "Holy fuck, Harlow!"

He frantically looked around and sobbed with relief when he saw her unharmed and in one piece.

Ryker helped his brother to his feet and handed him the change of clothes before wrapping a blanket around himself.

"You guys stay here and don't move," Harlow told them and walked around the crime scene. She found the tracks Kai and Orion had left behind when they first came upon the campsite. She envisioned the snow ahead of her as pristine and sent a ripple of magic out that erased the prints. She backtracked, erasing her own prints as she went. She moved around the campsite, cleaning up so there was only one set of tracks, and they were damaged enough that it would be hard to determine what type of animal was responsible. A few strands from a lion's mane vanished into the air with a snap of her fingers. Satisfied, she met up with the men, who watched her work with solemn expressions. They were all quiet as they made their way back to the Bronco. Harlow brought up the rear, erasing any evidence of their journey. She continued to do this once they were driving in reverse, bouncing over the ruts. The only tire tracks left in the partially frozen mud belonged to the hunter's truck.

Orion was sleeping on the backseat, covered in blankets.

Harlow sat up front in the middle, sandwiched between Ryker and Kai.

"What did you mean back there when you said that was your mess?" Ryker asked, and Harlow closed her eyes, unable to look at him. "Baby, is there something you're not telling me?"

She swallowed hard and clenched her fists on her lap. "I think I know what's wrong with Orion."

The inside of the Bronco became deathly quiet except for the soft snores coming from the backseat.

"Babe?" Ryker prompted, placing his hand on her left fist and unfurling it to lace his fingers with hers. "Talk to me."

Taking a deep breath, she squeezed his hand and told him everything. How Orion had died and she brought him back for Ryker because she loved him. She wanted him to know his brother after he had lost so much already. By the time she finished telling him, she was damn near hysterical because Ryker hadn't said a single word. He didn't have to. She could tell by the way he wrenched his hand away from hers and his jaw clenched that he was pissed.

The sky was beginning to lighten to the east, illuminating the craggy outline of Mount Sousa, when Ryker pulled up in front of Harlow's house. He didn't turn the ignition off or make any movements to get out of the car. Kai did, so Harlow could get out. He climbed back in, and before Kai shut the door, Ryker finally broke his angry silence.

"That was a big fucking secret to keep. What happened to being honest with each other?" He looked at her with such disgust that it took her breath away. Then he was driving off, and she had a horrible feeling that he was never coming back.

CHAPTER 10

The front door clicked softly closed behind her, and she leaned against it. Her entire body ached with exhaustion, and her eyes felt sticky from crying and lack of sleep. Unable to go any further, Harlow slid down the door and sat on the floor, her legs splayed out before her. Snow dripped off her boots, collecting in small puddles under her heels.

Sensing her distress, Mamoru appeared in the hallway. His nose twitched as he hopped toward Harlow and up onto her lap. She scooped him up and cradled him close. She had used a lot of magic that night, and just holding Mamoru, she started to recharge. He was her personal Energizer Bunny.

Eventually she pried herself off the floor, hung her parka up, and took off her wet boots. After putting on pajamas and making a cup of chamomile tea, she picked Mamoru up and brought him upstairs with her to her meditation area. She set her mug down on the table and set Mamoru on the floor before lighting a candle. Concentrating on that single flame, she mentally directed it to light the other candles around the room. One by one, they ignited, casting the room in soft light.

Harlow lay down on a yoga mat and draped a blanket over her legs. She stretched out on her back in savasana pose, arms extended out from her body with her palms facing the ceiling. Focusing on deeply inhaling and exhaling to fall into a meditative state wasn't working. Images of the man smoldering in the fire kept flashing through her mind, the smell buried in her nose. She struggled to push past the vivid memories, and eventually exhaustion won out. Harlow fell into a fitful sleep.

She was jerked awake when the front door slammed shut, rattling the house.

"Harlow, are you here?" her sister called out.

"Upstairs."

Soft footsteps sounded on the stairs, and seconds later, Taylor appeared. Her dark hair was pulled back in a ponytail, and she wore jeans with an old Sun and Moon Academy shirt. Taylor's eyebrows rose when she saw her sister on the floor with Mamoru tucked into the crook of her arm.

"I knew something was wrong," she said. "When you didn't show for lunch and weren't answering your phone, I just knew. What happened?"

Taylor sat down cross-legged on the floor next to her sister.

"Oh, shit. I forgot we were supposed to meet at Burger Bar today. Is it noon already?" Harlow looked around, disoriented and squinting to block the sun streaming in from the skylights.

"It's almost one. What, are you hungover or something?"

"No. Nothing like that." With a sigh, Harlow sat up, pulling the blanket over her lap. "I really screwed up."

"Harlow, I swear to goddess, will you just spit it out already? You're freaking me out!"

"Orion killed a man last night. Ripped an innocent human to shreds. And it's all my fault."

Taylor's mouth hung partly open, and her eyebrows had

practically disappeared into her hairline. "Are you serious right now?"

"I wish I wasn't. According to Kai Reynolds, Orion just snapped. I witnessed it. Orion tried to attack me. There was zero recognition in his eyes."

"Holy shit!"

"I told Ryker how I had reversed time to stop Orion from dying and how I think that's why he's not in control."

"And?"

Harlow rolled onto her back and sighed. "It didn't go well. What a disaster, and that poor man!" Tears spilled over and ran down the sides of her face into her hair. "I need to fix this, but I can't. A man is dead because of me, and the man I love can't even look at me."

Taylor stretched out next to her sister, and they lay side by side staring at the ceiling. Through the skylights it looked like a beautiful spring day. The sky was a clear blue, and the room was bathed in sunlight.

"Do you think there's information in the grimoire that will tell us how to help Orion, at least?" Taylor asked.

"Grandma keeps that guarded like it's the crown jewels. I don't know the spell to open the case. Do you?"

Taylor shook her head. "I think Gallad does."

"Well, he can't know what's going on."

Out of suggestions, Taylor stood up and forced Harlow to stand too, declaring she was starving. They went downstairs, and Harlow let Mamoru outside in the backyard where he immediately disappeared, his white fur blending in with the snow. Taylor helped herself and made a sandwich while Harlow made a cup of coffee. Her sister tried to cheer her up, but Harlow wasn't ready. Her emotions were too raw.

Soon after, Taylor left, and Harlow was alone again. She sat at the table, staring blankly at the backyard. The house was eerily quiet. She had become so used to having Ryker or Orion there, and without their big presences, her house was empty. Ryker was supposed to be a quick fling, but he had quickly assimilated into her life. His Harley Davidson coffee mug was in the dish drain, and his muscle-building protein shake mix was on top of the refrigerator. He liked to make one before he worked out at Get Buffed!, a gym owned by Oscar Vega, the sergeant at arms for SIN. Harlow hoped he would calm down, and they could find a way to see past her fuckup. She longed to reach out to him but decided to give him some time to cool off.

After a night spent tossing and turning, haunted by nightmares featuring the man Orion killed, Harlow woke up before her alarm went off. She managed to get a decent Wi-Fi signal and used her phone to search for any news on a body being discovered. Either he hadn't been found yet, or it hadn't hit the news. Harlow finished getting ready for work and walked to Coffee Haven, thinking fresh air was just what she needed to clear her head and reduce the puffiness around her eyes. Turns out that crying for almost twenty-four hours is hell on the face.

It was only her and Davis opening that morning. Davis had become an expert in sensing her mood, which made her wonder if he was slightly empathic like Willow, and he left her alone. They had worked together long enough to establish a rhythm. Around midmorning, Willow showed up, and she zeroed right in on Harlow.

"Can I see you in my office?" she asked her. Harlow followed the petite blonde to the back of the shop and into the small office. Willow shut the door. She didn't waste any time. "Holy fairies, girl! You're like a tornado of emotion. I felt it before I even stepped inside the shop. I'm surprised Sedona hasn't been over here to check on you. What is going on?"

Willow set her bag down on her desk on top of a stack of paperwork.

"I didn't realize. I thought I was suppressing."

"More like broadcasting. Are you going to tell me what's wrong?"

"Ryker and I are having some issues." Harlow looked down at the tops of her black boots, at the walls, at the pile of toys in the corner—everywhere but Willow's eyes. She knew the sensitive fae would be able to read more if they made eye contact. Willow sat on the edge of her desk, and Harlow felt her boss surveying her.

"It's more than that. You're spilling over with guilt, hurt, and fear, but I can also sense you're not ready to tell me. Is there anything I can do to help?"

Tears welled up in Harlow's eyes, and she blinked them away. Swallowing hard over the lump that had formed in her throat, she shook her head no. "I wish there was something. This is my burden to bear."

"Well, I can give you the rest of the day off. Paid. Go get a pedicure at VIP Nails or take a yoga class. Take care of you, okay? Davis and I can handle things here."

Harlow sniffed and wiped a stray tear off her cheek. "Thank you."

With that, she grabbed her coat and bag from the rack on the back of the office door and went out the side door into the alley. She didn't want customers to see her upset. Especially Irene Beckett and Biddie Half-Moon, who were holding court in the front of the shop.

Instead of dropping in for a pedicure or taking a yoga class, Harlow walked home, and as she approached her house, she was surprised to see Ryker's Bronco parked in her driveway. He was just coming down the steps from the porch, and he stopped when he saw her walking toward him. His hair was pulled back at the nape of his neck, revealing his face and making the shadows under his eyes more visible. A plain black duffel bag was over his shoulder.

"I was grabbing Orion's things," he explained.

Harlow shivered and crossed her arms over her stomach, like she was hugging her belly; his demeanor was so cold. "How is he?"

"He's fine right now and will stay at the clubhouse so we can keep an eye on him."

Harlow nodded and looked down at her foot as she kicked at a section of ice on the walkway. Steeling herself, she took a deep breath and looked back up, meeting his stormy blue gaze. "And how are you?"

He started to reach for her but pulled back. "I'm still mad at you. I understand why you did it. I just . . ." He trailed off and looked at her, softness seeping into his gaze. "I need some time. I need to figure out how to fix Orion. The little shit has been in my life for a little over a month, and I can't imagine him not in my life. Even though he's fucked up right now, he's here because of you."

"I'm going to find a way to fix him," Harlow promised, before Ryker walked away and got into his Bronco.

CHAPTER 11

$\mathcal{I}$t was the middle of April when the hunter's body, or what was left of it, was found. The elements and animals had apparently feasted on him. Harlow came across the news story during what had become her morning ritual of scouring the internet while having her first of many cups of coffee. She basically lived on coffee anymore, since sleep all but evaded her. Guilt haunted her like a specter. Now she knew the man's name. Knew he was a retired plumber who lived alone after his wife died. He was a grandfather. Because of her, this devoted family man was gone.

It was Sunday, and she was due at her grandparents' for more training. She went through the motions on autopilot: get dressed, feed Mamoru, brush teeth. She arrived at ten o'clock on the nose, and her grandfather opened the door. He frowned as he took in her appearance. Harlow knew she had lost more weight and didn't have much more to lose. Her leggings were loose, and she could count her ribs through her skin.

"Surely your broken heart must be on the mend soon? You're

young and will find love again," he said as he hugged her, placing a kiss on her cheek before stepping away.

Everyone thought Harlow was falling apart because of what they assumed was her breakup with Ryker. Very few knew what ate away at her from within. Now she understood Lady Macbeth being driven mad by the spot of blood on her hand. That stain never washed clean. Harlow had practiced magic she was warned against using and was paying the price.

Ryker hadn't disappeared from her life. They talked several times a week. He occasionally spent the night, and she savored those moments wrapped in his arms. They hadn't made love since that night and that was okay. She didn't deserve what he offered. Each night he stayed with her, someone with the MC kept watch over Orion. When Orion went hunting, he went with a group. The area was scouted and secured so no innocents could be harmed. He was getting worse, though.

"It's almost like he's two different people," Ryker had told her two nights earlier. He spooned her from behind and spilled his frustrations out, his breath tickling the hair by her ear. "One hour he's fine, and the next he doesn't know who I am and he's like a fucking feral beast."

Her heart broke all over again when she heard the pain in his voice.

"I'm so sorry." She rolled over in his arms to face him. "Will you ever forgive me?"

"Shhh, baby." Ryker kissed her forehead. "That's already done. You just need to forgive yourself."

That conversation resonated in her head as she walked down the hallway to the office where her grandmother was waiting. Harlow knew the only way to relieve herself of the guilt and to even begin to forgive herself—she needed to come clean.

"Good morning, Grandma," Harlow greeted her grandmother, who was sitting at the desk writing something down.

The doorbell rang, and Mathilde looked up, a confused expression on her face. "If you're here, who is that, I wonder?"

"I called a family meeting," Harlow answered.

"You did— What for?"

"You'll find out. We're gathering in the living room."

Mathilde rose from the chair and followed Harlow down the hall. As they drew closer, the murmur of voices became louder. Seated around the living room were Harlow's parents, sister, grandfather, and one non-family member: Ryker. He looked extremely odd, wearing his leather cut while sitting on a floral chair.

"What is he doing here?" her grandmother hissed from behind.

"Wait and see." Harlow remained standing while everyone else sat. She paced in front of them, wringing her hands together.

"In February, when Ryker and I went to Denver, I did something bad," Harlow began and didn't stop until she told them everything. When she finally finished, the only sound in the room was the creak of the chair as Ryker got up. He crossed the room and pulled her into a hug.

"It's because of him. He asked you to use your magic to save his brother! He's pulling you away from your family and making you do these things." Her grandmother stood up and pointed a finger at Ryker.

"That is not true!" Harlow straightened her spine, wiped tears from her cheeks, and squared off with her grandmother. "He didn't know—not until the night Orion killed the man. I am responsible. I made the decision. Yes, it was impulsive, but it was done out of love. I love Ryker and only wanted to lessen his pain."

At her admission, Ryker reached for her hand, and she held on tight. "This isn't about whether you think Ryker is good for me or not. He was angry at first, but he's been more than understanding. I'm struggling under the burden, and I asked you here for your help as family." Harlow looked at her grandmother. "Not as high priestess of the Luna Coven or as a member of the Court. But if you can't separate the two, and I need to be punished? So be it."

Ryker growled at that and pulled her against his side protectively.

Harlow's mom rose from where she had been sitting on the loveseat and crossed the room to stand in front of Harlow. "I'll do everything within my power to help you. I wish you came to us sooner."

"Yes, sweet pea, you're our daughter." Her father joined them, and he nodded at Ryker. "I can tell by the way you look at her that you love Harlow."

"I do. I don't have much, but she makes me want a better life —with her by my side."

"Mathilde, are you going to help our granddaughter or what?" Del's voice held a commanding tone. "Or are you going to continue to let her fade away before our eyes?"

"Fine. Only because this death and your use of magic happened outside of the wards, beyond the Court's jurisdiction. However, this Orion is unpredictable and still poses a threat to our town. He needs to be dealt with immediately."

Ryker tensed. Harlow felt his muscles stiffen, and a low growl rumbled deep in his chest.

"What do you mean, 'dealt with'?" he asked.

"That attitude won't win you any favors with me, young man," Mathilde snapped back at him. "Bring your brother here and we'll assess him."

Taylor spoke up then. She'd been quiet the entire time. "There's a darkness within him. Like death never left him."

"You knew about this?" Mathilde's voice raised an octave with shock. She looked between her two granddaughters with narrowed eyes, as if seeking out any more deception.

"I did," Taylor admitted softly. "I didn't want Harlow to get in trouble. I don't want to lose her. The Court can be harsh with its judgments, and she's already on probation."

Harlow moved away from Ryker and pulled her sister into a hug. Taylor gripped her back tightly, and they held each other for a long time.

"It's a good thing your sister and I have a connection to the dead," Harlow's mom spoke up. "Ryker, please bring Orion here. I won't let any harm come to him." At that statement, Aimi glared at her mother-in-law. "Isn't that right, Mathilde?"

Clearly outnumbered, Harlow's grandmother finally nodded in agreement. "Bring the boy here."

An hour later, Ryker arrived with Orion. Harlow was shocked at his appearance. She hadn't seen him since that fateful night, and he too had lost weight. His face was more angular, his cheekbones more pronounced. They stood out like sharp points above a scruffy beard. Whatever battle was raging within was taking a toll.

"Orion," Harlow cried out and rushed to hug him, but Ryker held a hand up to stop her. He had a firm grip on Orion's upper arm.

"Don't. He's hanging on by a thread."

Without any advance warning, Harlow thought out her intentions and snapped her fingers, freezing Orion in place. "Hurry. Now's the time to do this."

The urgency in her tone was unmistakable, and everyone jumped into action.

Harlow's mom and sister approached Orion's still form. He stared ahead, unblinking. He reminded Harlow of a figurine from Madame Tussauds wax museum. She had visited the one in Las

Vegas a few years ago when her dad was attending a golf course managers' conference. Mathilde retrieved the grimoire from the office and flipped through the fragile pages as quickly as possible. Harlow's dad and grandfather recited incantations while pouring a circle of salt around Orion.

Her mom explained that most likely Orion was stuck between both realms: the living and the dead. Each side struggled for dominance. She and Taylor were going to attempt to connect with the dead half and try to get it to release its hold. If not, an exorcism of sorts would have to be performed. The salt circle ensured that if they had to go that route, whatever energy escaped would be contained.

Following Aimi's instructions, Taylor placed a palm against Orion's left temple and Aimi placed her hand on the other side. Since they weren't blind like itakos of Japanese legend, they closed their eyes and began, their lips moving as they whispered, calling to the dead. Harlow and Ryker stood close by, hand in hand, anxiously watching and ready to react. Minutes ticked by, the grandfather clock documenting each passing second the only sound in the room. Mathilde had stopped researching and stood by, watching in fascination.

A dark mist began to seep out of Orion. It swirled around him like fog. Tendrils reached out and caressed Taylor's cheek, only to recoil back. The same happened when tendrils brushed against her mom's face. If it was seeking another host, the two itakos were incompatible. Taylor swayed slightly, but her mom clasped her hand. They stood a united force, drawing strength from each other, their combined chant growing louder as they expelled the darkness from Orion, who still stood unmoving and unblinking, as if he was already dead.

Suddenly the mist was free of Orion. Untethered, it hovered in the air like a storm cloud, roiling and angry, seeking escape but hitting invisible boundaries. The salt circle held, forming a protective dome. While it couldn't escape, magic could penetrate from the outside, and Mathilde stepped forward, her arms raised like she was conducting an orchestra. "I banish thee from this realm. You are not welcome here and are uninvited. Go back from whence you came. I mote it be!"

A rushing wind swirled around the room, knocking over picture frames and candles from surfaces. The coffee table was upended as the wind gathered speed. Mathilde's hair escaped the confines of her bun and blew around her face in a frenzy. She directed the wind, and it rushed forth, colliding with the mist.

Then it was gone.

Calm was restored, and no traces of the mist remained.

The spell on Orion released, he started to fall. Harlow's sister and mom grabbed his arms and steadied him. Blinking several times, Orion looked around the room in confusion at the upended furniture and items on the floor.

"What the fuck happened?" he asked his brother.

Whatever storm had resided in Orion's eyes was now gone. Ryker laughed and crossed the room, pulling his brother into a big bear hug, actually lifting him off the ground.

The joy was contagious, and Harlow felt a release. She was still burdened by the death of an innocent man, but at least Orion was back. His life wasn't forfeited either.

Harlow grinned when she noticed her grandmother nod approvingly at Ryker as he proceeded to clean up the items that had been tossed. She smiled even more when her grandmother applauded her mom and they left the room together.

"I'm proud of you, sweet pea. In fact, I'm proud of all my girls." Her dad gave her a hug and kissed the top of her head. "Are you hungry? I think it's time for lunch."

At the mention of food, Harlow's stomach growled. Her

appetite, suppressed by all of the stress and anxiety, had come surging back. "I could eat a horse!"

"I actually have. Not my favorite. I think it's an acquired taste," Ryker joked as he set the last picture frame upright.

Her father laughed and clapped Ryker on the back.

"I bet you have lots of stories," he said before he left, heading for the kitchen.

"Your family is pretty cool. You know that, right?" Ryker came up behind Harlow and wrapped his arms around her.

"Yeah, they're not perfect, but they're mine." Placing her hands over his, she leaned back against him. He rested his head on top of hers, and she melted into his embrace.

"I need to thank you." His voice vibrated against the back of her head. She turned in his arms so she could peer up at him, and he placed his hands on her hips.

"What for?"

"For saving my brother. Not once, but twice."

He leaned forward and captured her mouth in a kiss that almost incinerated her panties. He pulled her hips against his and growled in his throat as he deepened the kiss, his tongue teasing her lips before slipping between them. If they weren't standing in the middle of her grandparents' living room, she would have encouraged him to do more than kiss. A cough from behind broke through their lust, and Ryker lifted his head. His eyes were gold as he looked at her. She was warm from head to toe, and her lips felt swollen. Slowly they separated to see Orion grinning at them.

"Geez, get a room, you two.

Ryker flipped his brother off, and Harlow laughed at them as they continued to hassle each other on their way to the dining room. Her grandmother had conjured up a feast of epic proportions. A prime rib and a roast turkey sat simmering in their juices. Mashed potatoes, roasted vegetables, and fresh-baked rolls rounded out the feast. Her grandfather poured bourbon and wine for guests; even Taylor had a glass of red wine in front of her.

"Wow, how did you cook this so fast?" Orion asked, his eyes hungrily taking in the food.

"Magic, son," Harlow's grandfather replied with a wink.

Her family didn't publicly announce their acceptance of Ryker, but their actions said it all. Somewhere along the way, they must have seen her love for the lion shifter wasn't fleeting and his affection for her was real. Ryker had been considered a stray at one point, but as he told her father about his plans to build a house, that he was working so many jobs to save up money for land, she knew he was serious about putting down roots. She reached under the table and squeezed his thigh as he accepted another slice of prime rib from her grandmother.

"What?" He leaned over and nuzzled her neck, whispering the one-word question in her ear.

"Does the offer still stand?"

"What offer?"

"You, me, babies, a life together?"

His eyes flashed gold, and his fork dropped with a clatter onto his plate.

"Fuck yeah it does," Ryker growled, and the vibration raced along every nerve ending in her body. Turning her head, she met his lips, kissing him, sealing the promise. What started out as a one-night stand was going to be forever.

We hope you enjoyed this story in the Havenwood Falls world featuring a variety of supernatural creatures. Havenwood Falls is a collaborative effort by multiple authors. You might want to read E.J.'s other books in the Havenwood Falls universe:

Fate, Love & Loyalty (Havenwood Falls)
Fata Morgana (Havenwood Falls High)
Fated Beginnings (Legends of Havenwood Falls)

Books in the Havenwood Falls Sin & Silk series:

Taming the Beast by Nadirah Foxx
Plans Laid Bare by JD Nelson
Shift of Fate by Victoria Escobar
Stolen Wishes by Victoria Flynn
Damned Allure by Justine Winter
Savage Salvation by Kristie Cook
Dark Seduction by Michele G. Miller & R.K. Ryals
Soul Laid Bare by JD Nelson
Stray With Me by E.J. Fechenda
Chase the Flames by Desiree Lafawn
Flirting With Death by Nadirah Foxx

Also try the signature line, Havenwood Falls, the historical paranormal line, Legends of Havenwood Falls, and stories from the local supernatural college in Sun & Moon Academy.

Stay up to date at www.HavenwoodFalls.com

Subscribe to our reader group and receive free stories and more!

ABOUT THE AUTHOR

E.J. Fechenda has lived in Philadelphia and Phoenix, and now calls Portland, Maine, home. She is the Amazon bestselling author of the New Mafia Trilogy and in addition to working on the Ghost Stories Trilogy, she's a contributing author for the Havenwood Falls series. She has a degree in Journalism from Temple University, and her short stories have been published in *Suspense Magazine* and several anthologies.

You can find her on the internet here:

Facebook: https://www.facebook.com/EJFechendaAuthor

Twitter @ebusjaneus (https://twitter.com/ebusjaneus)

Tumblr: http://ejfechenda.tumblr.com/

Bookbub: https://www.bookbub.com/authors/e-j-fechenda

ACKNOWLEDGMENTS

There are so many people to acknowledge, especially the authors and readers who have made Havenwood Falls grow since the series launched in 2017. A huge shout-out to Kristie Cook for everything she does behind the scenes. Kristie, it's an honor to be a part of this journey with you. Thank you to fellow HWF authors who let me use their characters:

Amy Hale for the use of Kai Reynolds and Lawrence Mills.

C.J. Pinard for the use of Shayna Collins.

Randi Cooley Wilson for the use of Roman Bishop, Callie Montgomery, Irene Beckett, and Biddie Half-Moon.

Nadirah Foxx for the use of Monte and Hunter.

Amy Miles for the use of Fuzzbert and the Denver supernatural fight club.

Morgan Wylie for your beta reading and guidance on developing Mathilde Augustine as well as the use of a few other Augustines and Brock Blackstone.

My husband (Steve a.k.a. Bubba) deserves props for picking up the slack around the house when I lock myself away to write. He's also a great sounding board for ideas and providing insight into the biker world.

Finally, I need to thank my mom and dad for raising me to pursue my dreams and for their constant support. Just skip over the sex scenes, okay?

AN EXCERPT

~ A Havenwood Falls Sin & Silk Novella ~

HAVENWOOD FALLS

sin & silk

Chase the Flames

DESIREE LAFAWN

Chase the Flames (A Havenwood Falls Sin & Silk Novella) by Desiree Lafawn

He came for his mate. She can't fathom the idea of it. But the gods' will always wins.

Chevy Walker didn't come to Havenwood Falls to spread his wings or find a safe haven. No, he followed his natural instinct and the scent of his mate. He's got the bloodline, the power, and the money to make men and women fall at his feet, so why can't he bring one willful woman to heel? Chevy can play the nice guy. He hasn't broken the rules once—but even nice guys have their limits.

Hannah likes men, but not well enough to give up her freedom. Not like her ancestor, River, who had her power locked away in an amulet by a dusty old vampire. Hannah has her life in order and control of the heat and flames. She might not know the origins of her power, but she knows her future, and it does not include a cocky, controlling stranger—no matter that his voice gives her chills or how delicious he smells.

But Chevy's lineage could be the key to filling in the blank spaces in Hannah's history. She can choose to accept him as her mate willingly, or she can allow the madness to consume her until there's nothing left of either of them but a spark. For that seems to be the will of the gods.

CHASE THE FLAMES

BY DESIREE LAFAWN

I'd never witnessed a bar fight before. As someone in my position, I've had my share of struggles. I've fought for power, position, and authority. I've fought for my freedom in an oppressive establishment, but I'd never even seen a bar fight. Until now.

I'd also never seen a woman that small throw a punch hard enough to knock a guy twice her size clean off his feet. He went from towering over her as she sat in a chair, talking quietly with her young, curlyhaired companion, to flying through the air about eight feet away. It happened so fast, I might have missed the entire exchange if I hadn't already been staring at her. For reasons unrelated to her fight.

If the caterpillar from *Alice in Wonderland* reincarnated as a hippy, I was surely looking right at him. I'd been in Havenwood Falls for two days, and while the owner of the Haven Saloon wasn't the weirdest person I'd met so far, he certainly was one of the most interesting. Bent Brent—I couldn't get a read on him. Human for sure, but there was no way he didn't know that half his clientele was of the supernatural variety. Not when he had a shelf behind the bar, so low I almost couldn't see it, of bottles with labels that didn't have a damn thing to do with human consumption.

It couldn't be just the circle of smoke that wafted around his head that made him so mellow he didn't blink at the shocking violence happening right in front of him. That home roll clamped between his teeth might have been a special blend, but there wasn't a sticky on this earth that could make a man that relaxed. No, Bent Brent had the laid-back air of a man who had *seen some things*.

He didn't even quirk an eyebrow at the five-foot-nothing redhead who just sent a six-foot two-hundred-fifty-pound meat pinwheel somersaulting across the bar.

"You probably want to move over a hair." I barely heard the words as the barkeep mumbled them around the smoke still tucked between his lips.

The big guy landed right next to me, and if I'd been any slower, I would have taken a boot to the kneecaps as he sprawled haphazardly on his back, legs folded up against the bar wall and one arm flung over his face.

"Damnit, Hannah I wasn't ready." For a man who just had his innards reorganized, he sure had record recovery time. He was already on his feet and lumbering back to the table before I had time to blink.

"I wasn't aware there was a time frame I was supposed to operate in." The voice rang out merrily from across the room. Light, and maybe just the tiniest bit musical, if I wanted to admit my bias. "You said take my best shot. I took it." She walked toward where the man stood, mere feet from me, and patted the bigger man on the arm as she passed him. He flinched, but grinned good-naturedly.

"You're too little to hit so hard."

"I work out." She smiled back at him and laughed, making her way to my side of the room.

She reached the bar then, and the beast inside me, the one I shared my soul with, raised his head and eyed her hungrily. She was the one we were looking for. The one we came all the way here to find. This slip of a woman with fiery orange anime hair and a mean right hook was my mate.

I'd been following the pull for a few hundred miles. I would know her anywhere. That's the power of the mate bond. Genetics. Or at least that was what I'd found out, after a lifetime of thinking it was just heresy.

The mate bond existed, and every lie the elders of my caste had told me fell at our feet. They raised us to think we weren't like other shifters. No, our lineage was special; our sacred blood fragile. The elders paired us off to make sure we did everything in our power to perpetuate the continuation of our species.

At least that was the doctrine.

But I knew the truth now. And someday the rest of them would too, but before I could blow the conspiracy of the elders of my kind wide open, I had to come back with proof. Ranting like a lunatic and railing against the system about the medication we took to "stabilize our fragile blood and moody beasts" would not convince anyone to stop taking the meds. No. I had to find and bring them proof, and the only way to do that was to make an example out of myself. The only way to do that was to leave the family.

If it weren't for my best friend Baz, next in line for an elder position, I never would have made it. But here I was, clean from a lifetime of suppression drugs and feeling the pull of the mate bond for the first time in my life. It dragged me all the way across several states and up a mountainside. A feeling so strong I couldn't ignore it—neither could my beast. Dreams of smoke and ashes plagued me every night, but not nightmares. No, these dreams were filled with scents and sounds so pleasing I thought I would go crazy trying to find their source.

And then at the bottom of the mountain I'd caught her scent. The scent of my mate.

There was one for me, and she was right there in front of me. Everything I'd suffered in my thirty-some years of existence had led me right to this point. The lies, the grand plan, the breaking away to find out the truth—it all led up to this moment.

She was perfect.

"BB, can I get a . . ." Her words trailed off, and it was in that moment I knew. I didn't even have to see her sniff the air to tell the exact second she caught my scent. I wondered what I smelled like to her? I knew what she smelled like to me. Burning wood. Campfire. Fall leaves.

Sex.

That was there too, the underlying intent. When two mates found each other, the result could be explosive at first, as the desire to connect became overpowering. At least that's what I'd read. I'd been suppressed by the system of lies I was raised in, so I didn't have much time to process the information. But my rock-hard response had me believing that small bit of lore I'd uncovered before I'd made the move. Before I'd started my hunt.

I needed to touch her.

I also needed to not be a creep about it.

"What smells so good?" I didn't know who she was asking, but she was looking right at me, the dark pupils in her amber eyes expanding and contracting. Target acquired; I was in her sights. "Hello." She licked her lips, and my blood sang in response.

I'd done all of the research I could do with the limited resources available, but every bit of information I found pointed to how overwhelming and absolute the instant attraction and pull would be. I was prepared to exert iron control over my emotions and physical desires while I navigated the treacherous path of my mission. It didn't occur to me she would be just as affected as I was.

She touched my arm and I knew I would follow her anywhere.

"I'm Hannah. You're new here. What's your name? Where are you staying?" Those amber eyes studied me, and a light flickered there, a candle burning, nothing more.

That was a lot of questions to answer for someone who wasn't even looking me in the eye. I wondered if she expected my dick to answer, because her gaze moved down to my zipper and stuck there. If she didn't knock it off, I would give her something to look at, all right.

"I'm Chevy Walker, I'm from Arizona, and I'm staying at Whisper Falls Inn." Was she at the bar with anyone? Would she introduce me to them? What was her next move? Her hand was still on my arm, and I swear I could feel her heartbeat through her fingers and the fabric of my shirt—through the air even.

"The inn? That's close. Walking-distance close. That's good. Let's go there." And she turned toward the door, her hand still on my arm, steering me toward the exit with no other option but to follow her. Because I *had* to follow her. I inhaled her scent deep into my lungs and imprinted her on my body. The beast inside me did the same. This whole trip—this whole mission—was for her. It couldn't be this easy.

But it was that easy.

No one followed us out of the bar. No one raised an eyebrow at either of us as we left. I'd only been in Havenwood Falls for two days, and barring the sweet old ladies I met on my way into town, it seemed like a real *mind your own damn business* type of place.

But even a place where everyone minded their own probably wouldn't look the other way regarding two people boning in the street. Which is what *almost happened*. As soon as the old-fashioned batwing bar doors closed behind us, she was on me, hands grabbing, lips teasing. She went for my ear first, and I barely had time to catch her before she crawled up my body and stayed there, legs wrapped around my waist.

She weighed nothing.

She felt amazing.

For someone so slim and lithe, her curves were as soft as I thought they would be, and her small teeth nibbling on my earlobe froze the breath in my lungs. I had to lock my legs to keep from stumbling. The urgent need to possess her punched through me; I'd felt nothing so strong in my life. The books did not cover this kind of need. If I didn't strengthen my willpower, I would nail her in the street, and by the sounds coming out of her throat and the way her fingers dug into the flesh of my arms, Hannah would accept it willingly. The only other option was to hurry—or come in my pants like a first-timer.

I didn't have the heart or the willpower to push her away from me, so I did the next best thing I could think of. "Can you run?"

She grinned like a lunatic.

Turns out, she could.

There was no one at the inn, not in the hallways and not working the desk. Or at least it seemed that way as we escaped to the room, but most likely we were too wrapped up in each other to notice any innocent bystanders. I don't even remember taking the stairs, but I remember the sound of her small gasping breaths. Would she make the same sounds as we mated? I couldn't wait to find out. We made it, after an eternity of keeping our hands to ourselves, and I shut the door to the suite I rented, the lock clicking in place with a sinful finality.

Finally. I could touch her. Peel back the layers of clothing and savor with touch and taste the skin laid bare. There wasn't a spot of visible flesh I didn't want to bite, and some I couldn't see that I wanted to put my mouth on.

I don't know why I thought I would be in control.

She went straight for my pants. And by went straight for them, I mean she ripped them right down the seam on one side and tore them off. Hannah was *strong*, and a lesser man would have been terrified at the ferocity with which she disrobed me.

But I was not a lesser man, and there was nothing about Hannah I couldn't handle.

I appreciated her little gasp of happy surprise though, when she saw I went commando. Underwear was too restricting, and the less I had to remove before shifting the better. But she didn't know that. She knew none of it yet.

She will. My beast huffed in agreement.

"Hannah, slow down."

Her busy hands stopped briefly, and she uttered a small grunt of impatience. "Why?"

Why? I didn't know why. I couldn't shake off the lust-filled haze long enough to think of a single good reason she shouldn't do exactly what she wanted to me. But while I was fumbling for the words for what I was feeling, she dropped to her knees and slid her warm, moist mouth over the tip of my cock, stopping time completely.

"Hannah. Stop." I was as firm as possible, which was difficult with her mouth wrapped around my shaft and her hand cupping my balls. "Woman. Please."

Her only answer was to close her mouth and swallow, the muscles of her throat working to send me to the brink of destruction. In the space of a few mind-blowing seconds of pleasure, I realized two things: Hannah was a woman used to doing whatever she wanted whenever she wanted, as was obvious by her refusal to get off her knees and spit out my dick; and I was so turned on by the thought of taming her, I almost let her get away with it.

But I couldn't. Establishing dominance early was important for me and my beast. It was our nature to be alpha, and giving up the reins of control during sex was not acceptable—at least not the first time. Once we got to know our mate a little better, there would be plenty of time for experimenting, but right now she needed to stop or I was going to come, and Hannah would have made the first power move. Reaching down, I fisted my hands in her wild hair and tugged—not hard enough to sting, just enough to get her attention.

"Hannah, stop." I repeated my earlier order.

I don't know if she planned on obeying, but I broke her concentration enough for her to let go of me, and I hauled her back to her feet, spinning us both around, and pressing her back against the door so hard, she gasped with pleasure.

Oh? So Hannah likes to be handled a little bit. I squirreled the information away for future enjoyment.

"I'm the alpha here." I emphasized my point by gripping her hands and holding them above her head, my other hand resting lightly against her throat.

"Oh yes." The words were the barest of whispers. I bet she didn't even know she said them.

"I'm going to fuck you, Hannah, and you're going to look me in the eye while I do it." The scent of her arousal intensified—my filthy words pleased her. She wiggled against me but I didn't pull away—didn't allow her an inch of room. There was no way she didn't want me to pin her down, not with her eyes closed and that peaceful fucking smile on her face. Screw it. I'd held back for long enough. There was no one here to see or interrupt us. The beast inside me demanded I finish what the mate bond started. She was right there; no need to wait any longer. Hannah reared back

148

against my restraining hands not because she didn't want me touching her, but because she wanted to hang on to that role of being in control.

Not today. Not right now. She had to submit; my beast wouldn't allow anything else. We were just animals, after all.

"Tell me what you want me to do to you, Hannah. Tell me every dirty thing going on in that mind, right now." Still holding her hands immobile, I blazed a wet trail with my tongue from her ear to her collarbone, pausing at intervals to suck the flesh of her neck, bringing the blood to the surface. Leaving hickeys was juvenile. Maybe. But I would mark her as mine for anyone to see and to hell with the consequences. She was *my* mate. *Mine.* She wriggled, and I bit her firmly on the shoulder, wrangling a shriek of pleasure from her lips.

Hannah liked it rough. Excellent.

Purchase *Chase the Flames* where books are sold.

www.ingramcontent.com/pod-product-compliance
Lightning Source LLC
Chambersburg PA
CBHW051949170626
46808CB00007B/2536